STAR TREK®

VOLUME 13

Written by
MIKE JOHNSON

Art by
TONY SHASTEEN

Colors by
DAVIDE MASTROLONARDO

Letters by
ANDWORLD DESIGN and NEIL UYETAKE

Starship model reference provided by
MICHAEL WILEY

Series Edits by
SARAH GAYDOS

LEGACY OF SPOCK
Cover by Tony Shasteen

THIS MAY WELL BE THE STRUCTURE THAT MOST APPEALS TO ME ON ANY WORLD I HAVE VISITED.

IN COLOR AND DESIGN, IT WOULD NOT BE OUT OF PLACE ON VULCAN.
AS A YOUNG CADET I SPENT MANY HOURS WALKING ITS LENGTH IN QUIET CONTEMPLATION.

IT IS ONLY FITTING THAT I VISIT IT ONE LAST TIME.
IT IS UNLIKELY THAT I WILL HAVE THE OPPORTUNITY AGAIN.

I HAVE DELAYED MY DEPARTURE LONG ENOUGH.
MY SHUTTLE WILL BE EXPECTING ME.

THUS I BID FAREWELL TO SAN FRANCISCO.
AND TO STARFLEET HEADQUARTERS.
IT IS MOST CURIOUS TO WALK THE SAME PATHS I WALKED SO MANY YEARS AGO.
SO MANY DECADES AGO.
I HAVE MY ARRIVAL IN THIS ALTERNATE TIMELINE TO THANK FOR THE OPPORTUNITY.
AND ALTHOUGH THERE ARE SURFACE DETAILS THAT DIFFER, THE *SPIRIT* OF THE PLACE REMAINS THE SAME.
I HAVE NO DOUBT IT WILL THRIVE AS IT DID IN MY TIME.
AND I SUPPOSE, IN A SENSE...

...I WILL STILL BE HERE TO WITNESS IT.
IN THE FACE OF EXTINCTION, IT IS ONLY LOGICAL THAT I RESIGN MY STARFLEET COMMISSION AND HELP REBUILD OUR RACE.

AND YET YOU ARE IN A UNIQUE POSITION. YOU CAN BE IN TWO PLACES AT ONCE.
I URGE YOU TO REMAIN IN STARFLEET.

I HAVE ALREADY LOCATED A SUITABLE PLANET ON WHICH TO ESTABLISH A VULCAN COLONY, AND ASSIST IN THE FOUNDATION OF A NEW SCIENCE ACADEMY.

I ASK THAT YOU DO YOURSELF A FAVOR.
PUT AWAY LOGIC. DO WHAT FEELS *RIGHT*.

AS MY CUSTOMARY FAREWELL WOULD APPEAR SELF-SERVING, I WILL SIMPLY SAY...
...GOOD LUCK.

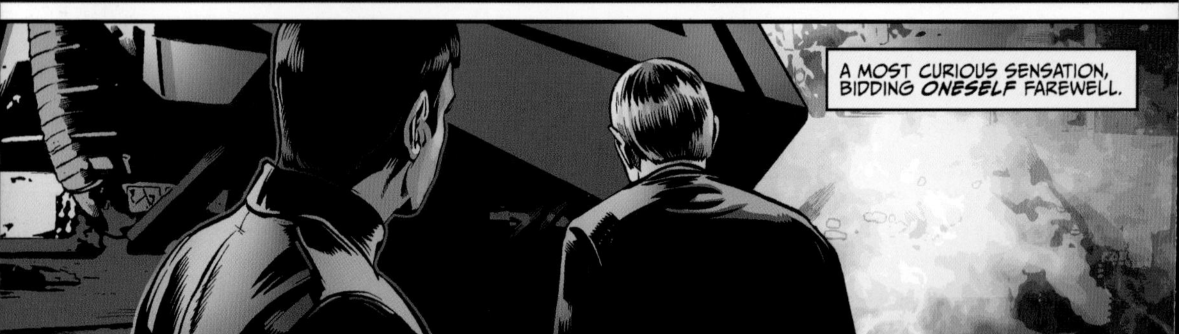
A MOST CURIOUS SENSATION, BIDDING *ONESELF* FAREWELL.

AS I LEAVE EARTH FOR THE LAST TIME, I AM REMINDED OF HOW FEW OF MY YEARS I HAVE ACTUALLY SPENT HERE.
STARFLEET UFP
BUT MY THOUGHTS SOON TURN FROM THE HOME OF MY HUMAN HALF...

...TO THE PLACE I CALLED HOME FOR SO MUCH OF MY LIFE.
OR, TO BE PRECISE, THAT HOME'S NEWEST INCARNATION.
AS MY SHUTTLE PASSES, IT OCCURS TO ME THAT AT THIS MOMENT I WOULD MOST LIKELY FIND ONBOARD TWO OLD FRIENDS...
NCC-1701
...NOW YOUNG AGAIN.
JIM, HOW CAN THOSE NUMBER-CRUNCHERS IN REQUISITIONS ONLY GIVE ME *HALF* THE SUPPLIES WE NEED TO SURVIVE THIS TRIP?
WHY WON'T YOU CALL ME "CAPTAIN"?

WHAT?
I GET IT, BONES. WE'RE OLD PALS!
BUT AT SOME POINT YOU'RE GOING TO HAVE TO ACCEPT THE SCARY TRUTH THAT I AM IN FACT—
I—
NCC-1701
HEY—
EARTH TO *CAPTAIN*—
YOU ALL RIGHT?
YEAH, I JUST...
SNAP
...NEVER MIND. REMIND ME WHAT YOU'RE COMPLAINING ABOUT?
WONDERFUL. SPACE-SICK ALREADY.

WHILE THE ENTERPRISE COMPLETES ITS REPAIRS, THE U.S.S. MUELLER HAS GRACIOUSLY VOLUNTEERED TO ESCORT ME TO MY DESTINATION.
THE CREW KNOWS NOTHING OF MY... UNIQUE... IDENTITY.
TO THEM I AM SIMPLY ANOTHER FORTUNATE SURVIVOR OF VULCAN'S DESTRUCTION.
THEIR SYMPATHY IS APPRECIATED BUT, IN MY CASE, MISPLACED.
IF ANYTHING, I DESERVE THEIR DISDAIN FOR MY FAILURE TO PREVENT THE DISASTER.
NCC-1475
DISDAIN I ANTICIPATE UPON MY IMMINENT REUNION WITH THE LAST OF MY PEOPLE.

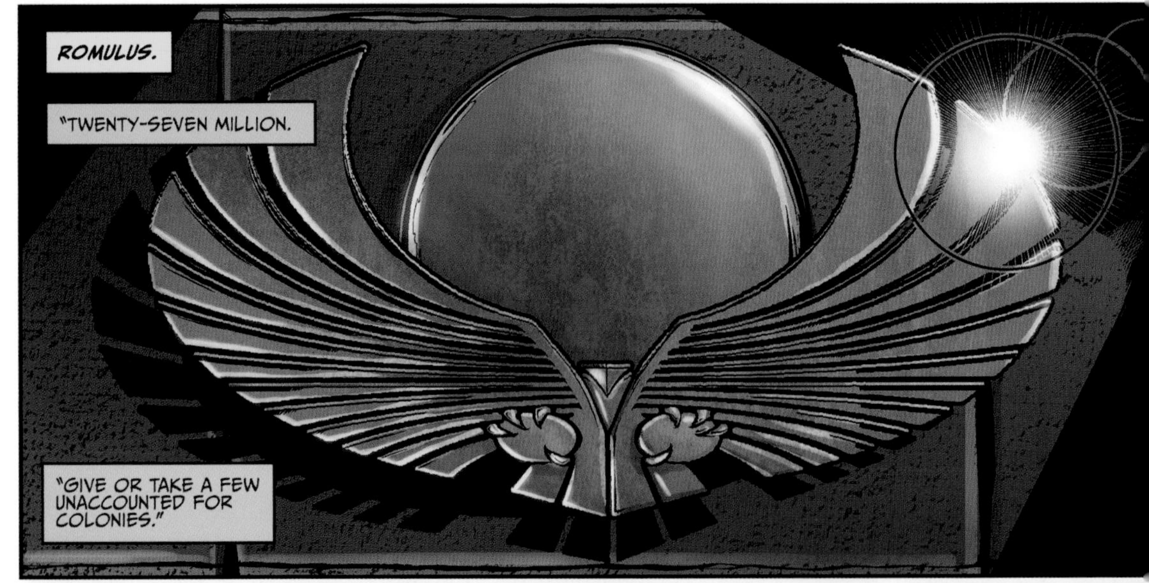
ROMULUS.
"TWENTY-SEVEN MILLION.
"GIVE OR TAKE A FEW UNACCOUNTED FOR COLONIES."

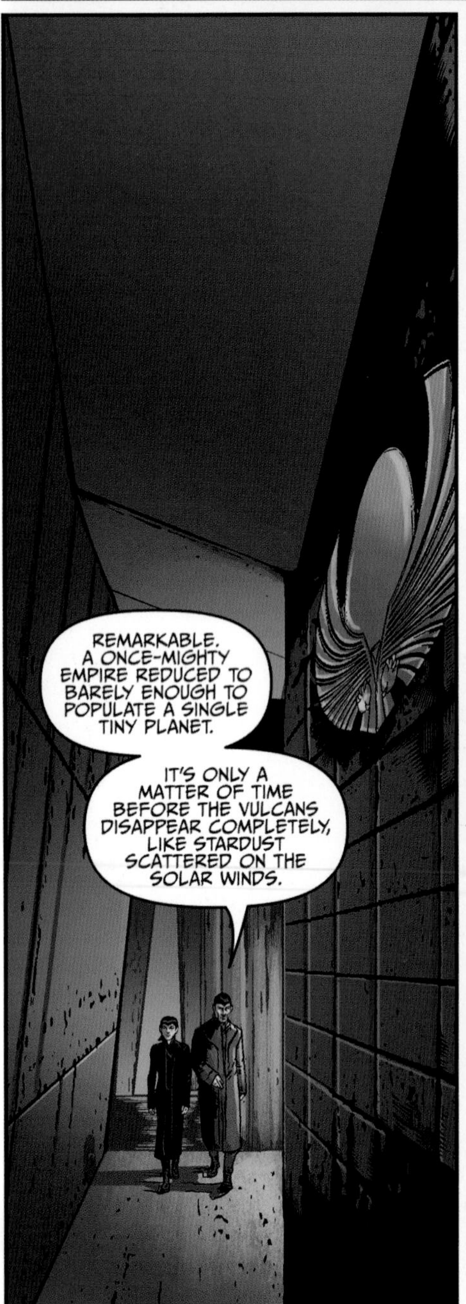
REMARKABLE. A ONCE-MIGHTY EMPIRE REDUCED TO BARELY ENOUGH TO POPULATE A SINGLE TINY PLANET.
IT'S ONLY A MATTER OF TIME BEFORE THE VULCANS DISAPPEAR COMPLETELY, LIKE STARDUST SCATTERED ON THE SOLAR WINDS.

WHY WAIT FOR THE WINDS TO DO OUR BIDDING, SENATOR?
OUR SPIES INSIDE THE FEDERATION REPORT THAT THE VULCANS ARE ALREADY MAKING PLANS TO REBUILD THEIR CIVILIZATION ON AN UNINHABITED WORLD.

WE WOULD BE WISE TO TAKE ADVANTAGE OF THIS REMARKABLE OPPORTUNITY.
OUR ANCIENT TIES TO THE VULCAN RACE SHOULD NOT DISSUADE US FROM EXTINGUISHING THE FEW THAT ARE LEFT.

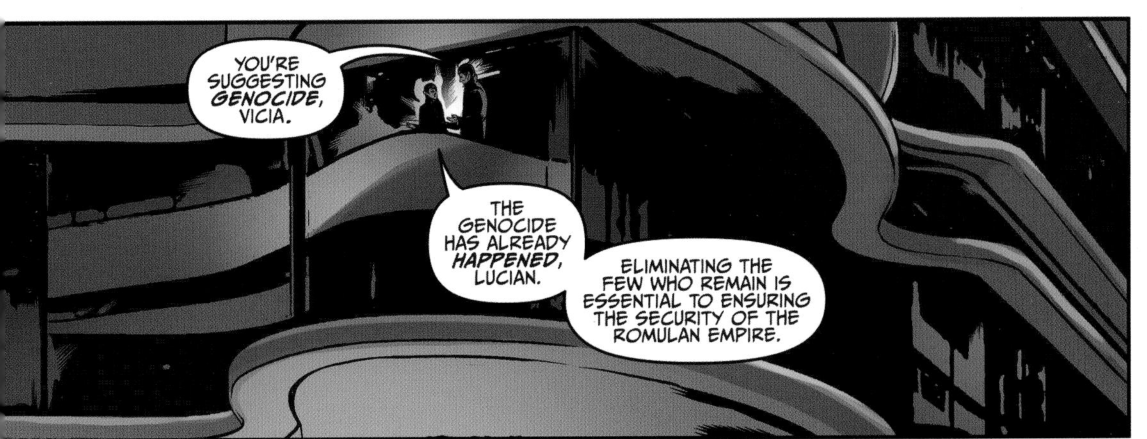
YOU'RE SUGGESTING GENOCIDE, VICIA.
THE GENOCIDE HAS ALREADY HAPPENED, LUCIAN.
ELIMINATING THE FEW WHO REMAIN IS ESSENTIAL TO ENSURING THE SECURITY OF THE ROMULAN EMPIRE.

VULCAN WAS DESTROYED BY ROMULANS OPERATING WITHOUT THE AUTHORITY OF OUR GOVERNMENT.
DO YOU THINK THAT MAKES A DIFFERENCE TO THE VULCANS?
WHEN THEY HAVE REGAINED THEIR STRENGTH, THEIR SOLE PURPOSE WILL BE THE DESTRUCTION OF THIS WORLD.

BY WHAT MEANS? THE LAST REMAINING MOLECULES OF THE RED ELEMENT USED TO DESTROY VULCAN ARE NOW IN OUR POSSESSION.
BARELY ENOUGH TO DESTROY A CITY, MUCH LESS A PLANET.

AND IF WE ALLOW THE VULCANS TO SURVIVE? WE ALREADY KNOW THAT THEY WILL ONE DAY INVENT THE ELEMENT.
NOW THEY WILL BE INCLINED TO DO SO EVEN FASTER THAN BEFORE.

THE CHOICE IS SIMPLE, LUCIAN.
A FEW MILLION VULCAN LIVES TO SAVE BILLIONS OF ROMULANS.

I FIND MY THOUGHTS OFTEN TURN NOW TO ENDINGS.
U.S.S. MUELLER
SHOULD I INDEED SPEND THE REST OF MY DAYS WITH THE VULCANS, THIS MAY VERY WELL BE THE LAST TIME I AM ABOARD A STARFLEET VESSEL.
LIKE MANY THINGS IN THIS ALTERNATE TIMELINE, IT IS AT ONCE MARKEDLY DIFFERENT IN SOME ASPECTS...
...AND UTTERLY FAMILIAR IN OTHERS.
MY SON.

TO CALL YOU SO IS ACCURATE, IS IT NOT?
IF NOT IN THE STRICTEST SENSE, THEN IN THE SPIRIT OF IT.
INDEED... SAREK.
I WAS PLEASED TO HEAR THAT YOU WERE ONBOARD. I DID NOT WISH TO INTRUDE ON YOUR PRIVACY, BUT I HOPED WE WOULD ENCOUNTER EACH OTHER AT SOME POINT.
I MADE CERTAIN OF IT.
IT IS NOT OFTEN THAT A FATHER ENCOUNTERS TWO VERSIONS OF HIS SON IN ONE LIFETIME.
NOR A SON HIS FATHER.
I AM PLEASED TO SEE YOU WELL.

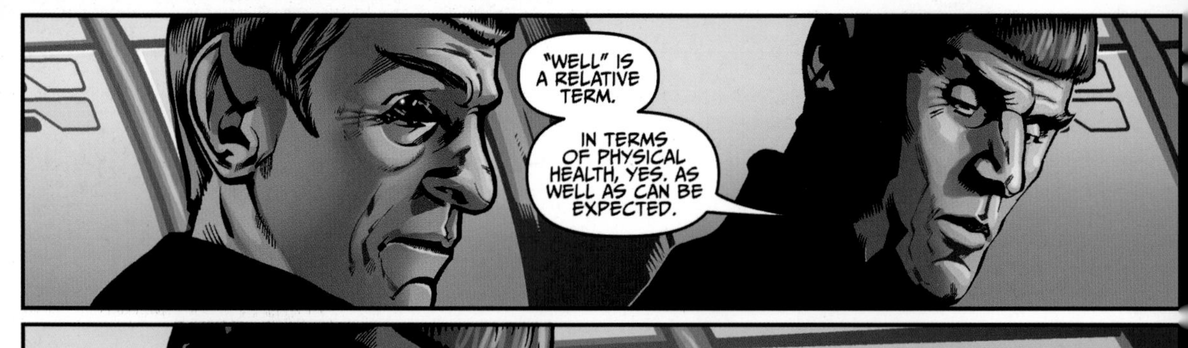
"WELL" IS A RELATIVE TERM.
IN TERMS OF PHYSICAL HEALTH, YES. AS WELL AS CAN BE EXPECTED.

BUT THE BURDEN I FEEL—
—THE BURDEN ALL *VULCANS FEEL*—
—LIES HEAVILY UPON ME.

IT IS MY HOPE THAT OUR REUNION WITH THE REST OF OUR PEOPLE WILL RESULT IN AN EASING OF THAT BURDEN FOR YOU.
TOGETHER WE CAN BEGIN TO REBUILD WHAT WE HAVE LOST.

AH YES.
"WE."
I MUST CONFESS, SPOCK, THAT CURIOSITY WAS NOT MY ONLY MOTIVE FOR MEETING WITH YOU.

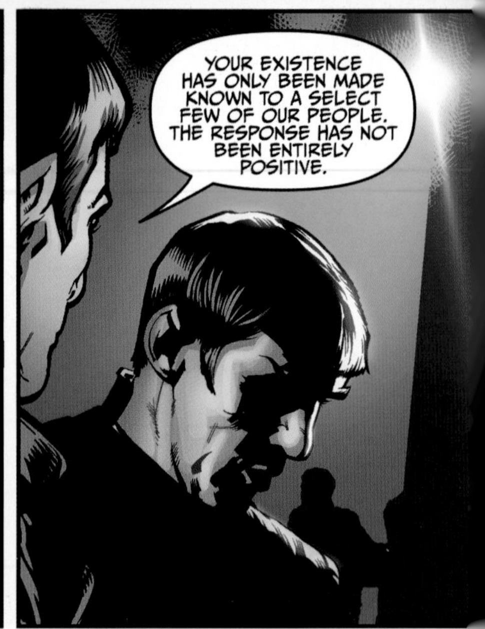
YOUR EXISTENCE HAS ONLY BEEN MADE KNOWN TO A SELECT FEW OF OUR PEOPLE. THE RESPONSE HAS NOT BEEN ENTIRELY POSITIVE.

AS I EXPECTED.
IN MY INITIAL CONTACT WITH THE SURVIVING ELDERS I RELAYED ALL RELEVANT FACTS REGARDING THE CAUSE AND EFFECTS OF MY ARRIVAL IN THIS TIMELINE.
IT IS LOGICAL THAT SOME WOULD SEE ME AS RESPONSIBLE—AT LEAST IN PART—FOR WHAT HAPPENED TO OUR HOMEWORLD.

MORE THAN SOME.
THAT IS WHY I WOULD ADVISE YOU *NOT* TO PARTICIPATE IN THE UPCOMING CONVOCATION.

I SEEK ONLY TO PROVIDE WHAT ASSISTANCE I—
SPOCK.
I AM ASKING YOU AS A FATHER.
CONSIDER A DIFFERENT PATH.

I DO NOT UNDERSTAND.
IS MY PLACE NOT WITH MY FELLOW VULCANS, PARTICULARLY AT THIS DIFFICULT TIME?

THAT REMAINS TO BE SEEN...

WE RENDEZVOUS WITH THE VULCAN FLEET IN ORBIT AROUND THE BARREN PLANET *REGULA 1* IN THE MUTARA SECTOR.
MY FATHER HAS OFFERED NO FURTHER EXPLANATION FOR HIS SUGGESTION THAT I AVOID PARTICIPATION IN THE ASSEMBLY TO COME.
I REMAIN UNCONVINCED THAT HIS APPREHENSION IS ANYTHING OTHER THAN THE RESULT OF HIS RECENT TRAUMA.
AND YET, AS WE JOIN OUR BRETHREN ABOARD THE FLAGSHIP *FORGE OF SURAK*, I CANNOT HELP BUT HEAR THE ECHO OF HIS WORDS.
AN ECHO NOT OF PARENTAL CONCERN...

...BUT OF WARNING.
IT WAS NOT AT RANDOM THAT WE CHOSE A LIFELESS PLANET FOR OUR PLACE OF GATHERING.
YES, IT IS SAFELY WITHIN THE BOUNDARIES OF FEDERATION SPACE, AFFORDING US THE SECURITY WE NEED AT THIS MOST CATASTROPHIC TIME.
BUT IT IS ALSO ENTIRELY SYMBOLIC OF THE TASK BEFORE US.
WE SEEK A NEW WORLD UPON WHICH TO ENSURE THAT THE LIFE OF THE VULCAN RACE WILL CONTINUE.
UNITED FEDERATION OF PLANETS

GIVEN THAT NO OTHER HABITABLE PLANETS EXIST WITHIN OUR HOME STAR SYSTEM, OUR ONLY OPTION IS TO CONSIDER OTHER WORLDS LIGHT-YEARS AWAY.
40 ERIDANI A

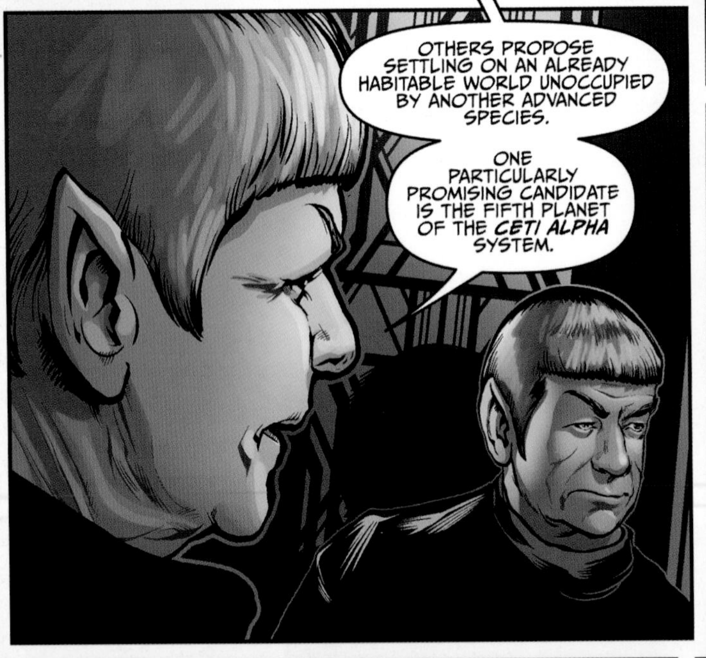
THERE ARE THOSE OF US WHO PROPOSE THAT WE FIND A PLANET MUCH LIKE THE ONE AROUND WHICH WE NOW ORBIT, AND EMBARK ON A PROCESS OF *TERRAFORMING* TO CREATE A NEW HOME.
OTHERS PROPOSE SETTLING ON AN ALREADY HABITABLE WORLD UNOCCUPIED BY ANOTHER ADVANCED SPECIES.
ONE PARTICULARLY PROMISING CANDIDATE IS THE FIFTH PLANET OF THE *CETI ALPHA* SYSTEM.

ELDER, IF I MAY INTERJECT—

AH. SPOCK.
I ATTRIBUTE YOUR WILLINGNESS TO *INTERRUPT* TO YOUR HALF-HUMAN NATURE.

THE COUNCIL WAS DUE TO ADDRESS YOUR UNIQUE SITUATION SHORTLY. YOU MAY AS WELL TELL US WHAT YOU HAVE TO SAY NOW.

THANK YOU FOR YOUR CONSIDERATION. AS THOSE IN THIS ROOM KNOW, I ARRIVED HERE FROM ANOTHER TIMELINE SEVERAL DECADES IN THE FUTURE.
I HAVE SWORN NOT TO INTERFERE IN THE COURSE OF THIS TIMELINE, EXCEPT WHERE NOT DOING SO WOULD HAVE CATACLYSMIC CONSEQUENCES.

SUCH IS THE CASE WITH *CETI ALPHA V*.
TO ESTABLISH A VULCAN COLONY THERE WOULD DOOM—

YOUR OPINION IS NOTED, SPOCK.
BUT YOU WERE NOT ASKED HERE FOR YOUR COUNSEL.

YOU ARE HERE TO SUBMIT TO THE *JUDGMENT* OF THE ELDERS OF VULCAN.
OVER THE OBJECTIONS OF YOUR FATHER, I SHOULD ADD.

I AM SORRY, MY SON.

HAVING TAKEN INTO ACCOUNT THE NATURE OF YOUR ARRIVAL FROM AN ALTERNATE TIMELINE INTO THIS ONE...
...AND CONSIDERING THE EVENTS THAT FOLLOWED...
...IT IS THE JUDGMENT OF THIS COUNCIL THAT YOU BE STRIPPED OF YOUR CITIZENSHIP AND PROHIBITED FROM CONTACT WITH OTHER MEMBERS OF YOUR RACE.
FROM THIS MOMENT ON, SPOCK...
...IN THESE EYES OF OUR PEOPLE...
...YOU ARE ***NO LONGER VULCAN.***

THE KLINGON PRISON PLANET *RURA PENTHE*.
KRAKK
⟨TELL US, DOG.⟩*
⟨TELL US MORE OF THIS FUTURE YOU CAME FROM. SHARE ITS SECRET WITH US.⟩
*TRANSLATED FROM KLINGON.
WHAKK
⟨YOUR OTHER ROMULAN FRIENDS ESCAPED AND LEFT YOU BEHIND.⟩
⟨WORD IS THEY'RE ALL DEAD NOW.⟩
KRUNCH
⟨BUT YOU DON'T GET TO JOIN THEM.⟩
⟨NOT YET.⟩

<YOU'VE STILL GOT **YEARS** TO—>
-HURRCH-
COME, BROTHER. ON YOUR FEET.
WE ARE FINALLY LEAVING THIS PLACE. **NERO** MAY WELL BE DEAD...
...BUT OUR **MISSION** REMAINS THE SAME.

DECADES AGO.
ANOTHER TIMELINE.
ANOTHER VULCAN.
"LAST CHANCE, MR. SPOCK."

ARE YOU SURE YOU DON'T WANT TO STAY HERE? YOU'VE BEEN AWAY FROM HOME FOR QUITE AWHILE.
MY RESPONSIBILITIES REST WITH STARFLEET, CAPTAIN.
I HAVE EVERY INTENTION OF FULFILLING THEM.

YOUR DEDICATION IS ADMIRABLE.
BUT I'D UNDERSTAND IF YOU WANTED MORE TIME AT HOME.

HUMANS' USE OF THE WORD "HOME" CARRIES WITH IT A SENTIMENTAL MEANING TO WHICH VULCANS ARE IMMUNE.
I WAS BORN ON VULCAN, YES. BUT I HAVE NO EMOTIONAL ATTACHMENT TO IT.

"NO EMOTIONAL ATTACHMENT"?
YOU DAMN NEAR KILLED YOUR CAPTAIN YESTERDAY THANKS TO THAT PON FARR BUSINESS!
I'D HATE TO SEE YOU WHEN YOUR EMOTIONS REALLY FLOW!

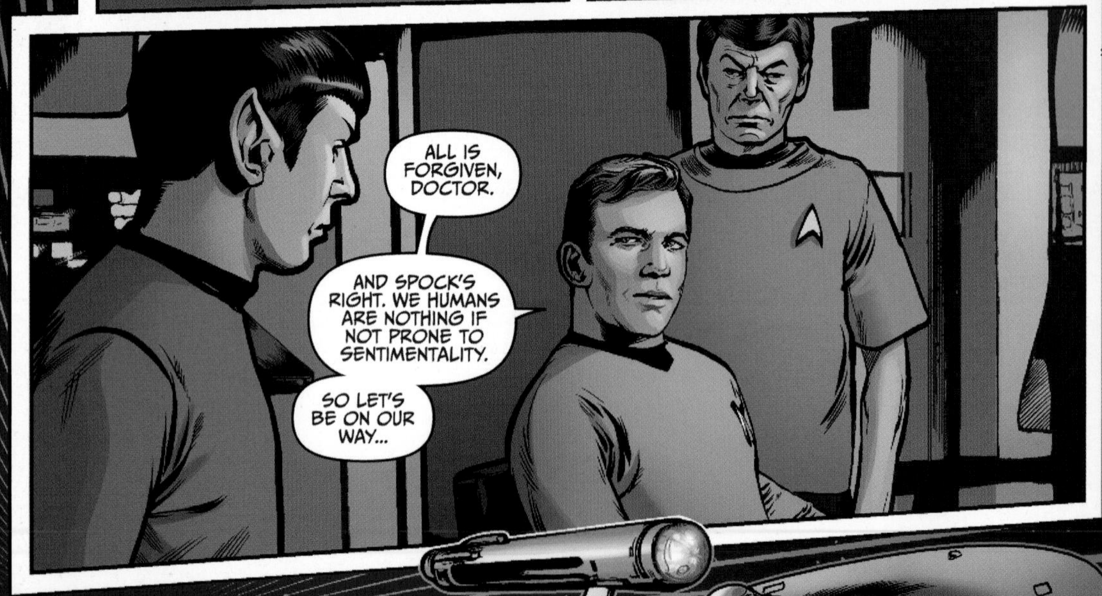

ALL IS FORGIVEN, DOCTOR.
AND SPOCK'S RIGHT. WE HUMANS ARE NOTHING IF NOT PRONE TO SENTIMENTALITY.
SO LET'S BE ON OUR WAY...

"...AND SAVE GOODBYES FOR ANOTHER TIME."

U.S.S. ENTERPRISE NCC-1701

AND SO I LEFT THE VULCAN PEOPLE BEHIND.

AGAIN.

AS I LEAVE THEM BEHIND *TODAY.*
THIS TIME, THE CHOICE IS NOT MY OWN.

MY FATHER--
--MY FATHER IN THIS *NEW TIMELINE*--
--ASKED TO ESCORT ME OFF THE VULCAN CAPITAL SHIP.
I AM SORRY IT HAS COME TO THIS, SPOCK.
I PRESSED THE ELDERS TO CONSIDER OTHERWISE, BUT THEY REMAINED CONVINCED THAT YOU ARE IN PART RESPONSIBLE FOR OUR HOMEWORLD'S DESTRUCTION.

WE MAY NOT AGREE WITH THEIR LOGIC, SAREK, BUT I UNDERSTAND IT.
THERE ARE WORSE FATES THAN *EXILE.*
WHERE WILL YOU GO?

SOMEWHERE I CAN HELP TO ENSURE THE SAFETY OF ALL VULCANS, WHETHER MY ASSISTANCE IS REQUESTED OR NOT.

SHOULD WE NOT MEET AGAIN, SAREK, YOU HAVE MY GRATITUDE.
I ONLY ASK THAT YOU DO ALL YOU CAN TO CONVINCE THE ELDERS THAT CETI ALPHA V IS NOT A VIABLE LOCATION FOR A NEW COLONY.
I WILL DO WHAT I CAN. FAREWELL...

...MY SON...

"YOUR MEETING WITH THE OTHER VULCANS WAS SURPRISINGLY BRIEF, MR. SPOCK."

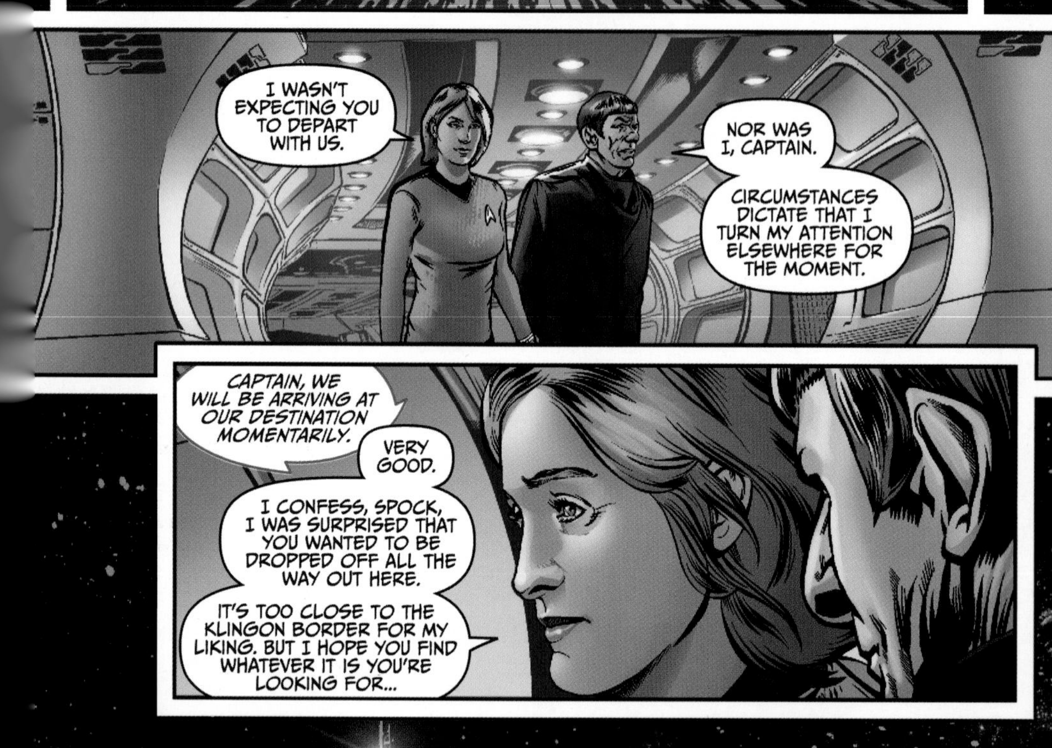
I WASN'T EXPECTING YOU TO DEPART WITH US.
NOR WAS I, CAPTAIN.
CIRCUMSTANCES DICTATE THAT I TURN MY ATTENTION ELSEWHERE FOR THE MOMENT.
CAPTAIN, WE WILL BE ARRIVING AT OUR DESTINATION MOMENTARILY.
VERY GOOD.
I CONFESS, SPOCK, I WAS SURPRISED THAT YOU WANTED TO BE DROPPED OFF ALL THE WAY OUT HERE.
IT'S TOO CLOSE TO THE KLINGON BORDER FOR MY LIKING. BUT I HOPE YOU FIND WHATEVER IT IS YOU'RE LOOKING FOR...

"...AT DEEP SPACE STATION K-7."
K7

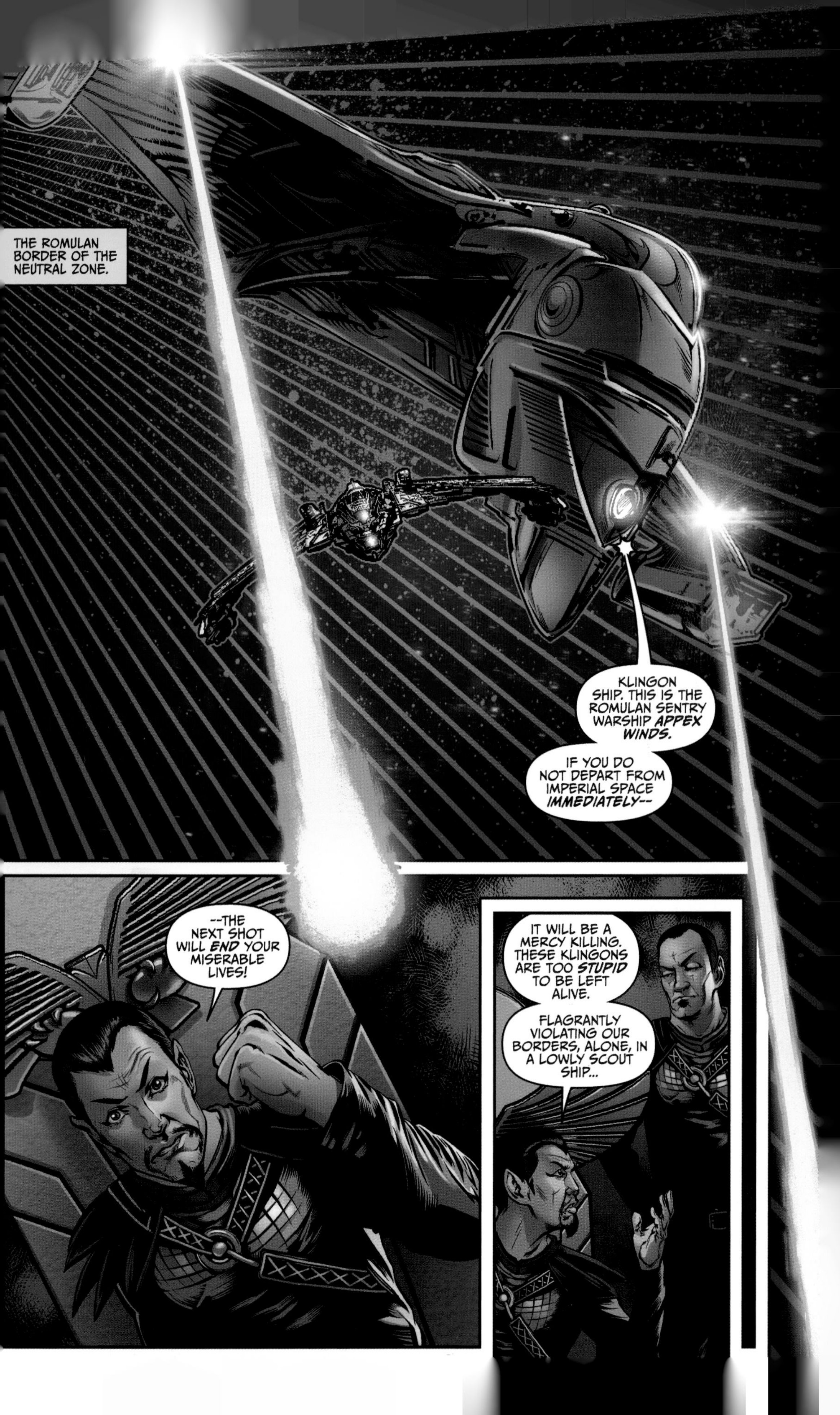
THE ROMULAN BORDER OF THE NEUTRAL ZONE.
KLINGON SHIP. THIS IS THE ROMULAN SENTRY WARSHIP *APPEX WINDS.*
IF YOU DO NOT DEPART FROM IMPERIAL SPACE *IMMEDIATELY--*
--THE NEXT SHOT WILL *END* YOUR MISERABLE LIVES!
IT WILL BE A MERCY KILLING. THESE KLINGONS ARE TOO *STUPID* TO BE LEFT ALIVE.
FLAGRANTLY VIOLATING OUR BORDERS, ALONE, IN A LOWLY SCOUT SHIP...

CAPTAIN, THEY'RE HAILING US, BUT NOT IN KLINGON--
--AND WE DON'T NEED THE TRANSLATORS--
THEY'RE SPEAKING PERFECT ROMULAN!
ONSCREEN!
KLINGON AGGRESSORS! IDENTIFY YOURSELVES!
NO AGGRESSION IS INTENDED.
OUR ONLY INTENTION, AFTER A VOYAGE LONGER THAN YOU CAN IMAGINE...
...IS TO FINALLY COME HOME.

THE MORE TIME I SPEND IN THIS NEW TIMELINE, THE MORE I NOTICE DIFFERENCES THAT GO BEYOND THOSE CAUSED BY NERO'S ARRIVAL.
LOCATIONS I HAVE VISITED BEFORE, LIKE THIS ONE, APPEAR SIMILAR IN MOST RESPECTS. BUT THERE ARE SMALL CHANGES THAT I SUPPOSE ARE INEVITABLE GIVEN THE NATURE OF INFINITE REALITIES.

I REMEMBER THE STRUCTURE OF THIS STATION, BUT THE DECOR HAS CHANGED.
I RECOGNIZE SPECIES, BUT NOT THE CLOTHES THEY WEAR.

AND YET THE MEMORIES ARE AS CLEAR AS THE DAY THEY FIRST FORMED.
SAMMY'S BODEGA
OH CHEKOV, ISN'T IT *ADORABLE?*

VAT ARE YOU GOING TO DO WITH EET?
I'M GOING TO GIVE IT A *HOME!*

THAT CREATURE MUST FIRST PASS THROUGH THE SHIP'S QUARANTINE PROTOCOLS.

I KNOW, COMMANDER.
AND AFTER THAT YOU CAN DEBRIEF IT ON ALL OF THE SHIP'S RULES AND REGULATIONS!

IT WAS THE PROLOGUE TO AN EVENTFUL DAY.
AND IT IS THE ORIGINAL INSTIGATOR OF THOSE EVENTS...

...WHOM I HOPE TO FIND HERE TODAY.

ROMULUS.
WHERE IS IT?

IT'S RIGHT IN FRONT OF US, TOO SMALL TO SEE WITH THE NAKED EYE.
BUT ITS POWER IS *INDISPUTABLE.*

THE LAST REMAINING MICROSCOPIC PARTICLES OF THE *SUBSTANCE* THAT DESTROYED VULCAN.
IT IS *DECAYING.* THERE IS LESS AND LESS OF IT EVERY DAY. BUT THERE REMAINS ENOUGH TO WIPE OUT THE VULCAN SURVIVORS.

THEN WE MUST NOT DELAY.
THE LATEST REPORT FROM OUR SPIES INDICATES THAT THE VULCANS ARE EN ROUTE TO *CETI ALPHA V.*
WE WILL MEET THEM THERE.

HAS PROVED SUCCESSFUL.
IT WAS LOGICAL THAT THE MAN I SEEK WOULD ALSO EXIST IN THIS TIMELINE, AND FREQUENT THE SAME ESTABLISHMENTS.
AND THUS I AM REACQUAINTED...

...WITH *CYRANO JONES.*
DID YOU NOT HEAR ME THE FIRST FIVE TIMES?
THIS IS *ANTAREAN* GLOW WATER! I'LL NOT CUT MY PRICE FOR SUCH A RARE COMMODITY!
MR. JONES?

MISTER JONES? ONLY THE AUTHORITIES CALL ME THAT.
I'M CYRANO TO EVERYONE ELSE.

AND IF YOU KNOW WHO I AM, YOU MUST KNOW MY REPUTATION AS THE MOST HONORABLE BUSINESSMAN IN THE GALAXY. WHAT CAN I DO FOR YOU, MY DEAR VULCAN FRIEND?
OR ARE YOU UNHAPPY WITH A PREVIOUS PURCHASE WHOSE DETAILS I DO NOT RECALL BUT AM CERTAIN WERE COMPLETELY ON THE LEVEL?

I ASSURE YOU, CYRANO, THAT MY ONLY INTENTION IS TO AVAIL MYSELF OF YOUR...
...UNIQUE...
...SERVICES.
WELL, IN THAT CASE...

WHAT TYPE OF SERVICE DO YOU REQUIRE?
TRANSPORT ABOARD YOUR VESSEL.
TO ROMULUS.

HOW DARE YOU, SIR, ASSUMING I WOULD VIOLATE ROMULAN SPACE IN SUCH A CAVALIER MANNER!
YOU ARE NO DOUBT WELL AWARE THAT ONLY SMUGGLERS HAVE ACCESS TO THE EMPIRE'S TRADE ROUTES WITHOUT OFFICIAL AUTHORIZATION!

I CAN AFFORD ANY PRICE YOU WISH. DOUBLED.
...ANY?
...DOUBLED?

YOU HAVE MY UNDIVIDED ATTENTION, GOOD SIR!
AND MIGHT I ADD MY MOST SINCERE CONDOLENCES OVER THE LOSS OF YOUR HOMEWORLD!

IT IS FORTUNATE THAT I DO NOT HAVE TO COMPEL HIS AGREEMENT BY INFORMING HIM THAT I COME FROM AN ALTERNATE TIMELINE IN WHICH HIS RECENT SALE OF A TRIBBLE TO STARFLEET OFFICERS RESULTS IN AN INFESTATION OF THEIR SHIP, AND HIS IMMINENT ARREST.
THANK YOU.

NOT TO MENTION THAT I'M OVERDUE FOR RESUPPLYING MY STOCKS OF ROMULAN ALE. I DO SO ENJOY A MUTUALLY BENEFICIAL ARRANGEMENT!
TELL ME, WHERE EXACTLY WOULD YOU LIKE TO BE DELIVERED?

I HAVE BUSINESS IN THE CAPITOL.

THE ROMULAN SENATE.
THE TALE YOU TELL IS AS UNBELIEVABLE AS IT IS ASTONISHING.

AND YET THE EVIDENCE CANNOT BE DENIED.
YOUR PRESENCE BEFORE US IS A *GIFT.*

IT IS THE JUDGMENT OF THE SENATE THAT YOUR IMPERIAL CITIZENSHIP BE CONFIRMED, AND THAT, DESPITE YOUR CIVILIAN STATUS, YOU BE ACCORDED ALL BENEFITS AND RESPECT DUE *SOLDIERS OF ROMULUS.*
WE HAVE MUCH STILL TO LEARN OF YOUR *PAST,* ALL FOR THE BENEFIT OF THE EMPIRE'S *FUTURE.*

WELL, SENATOR LUCIAN...

...IT APPEARS WE'VE FOUND THE PERFECT AGENTS TO ENSURE OUR PLAN'S SUCCESS.

WELCOME TO ROMULUS!
FIRST TIME HERE, MR. SPOCK?
NO...
...AND YES.
HOW WONDERFULLY MYSTERIOUS!
WELL, LET'S SETTLE UP ACCOUNTS...

"...AND SEE YOU SAFELY TO YOUR DESTINATION."

IT IS STRIKING TO WITNESS THIS WORLD ALIVE AGAIN.
I WALK AMONG THE FOREBEARS OF THE LAST ROMULAN GENERATION AS I KNEW IT IN MY OWN TIME.

I SEEK ONE OF THOSE FOREBEARS IN PARTICULAR.
"WELL, MR. ...SPOCK, IS IT?"

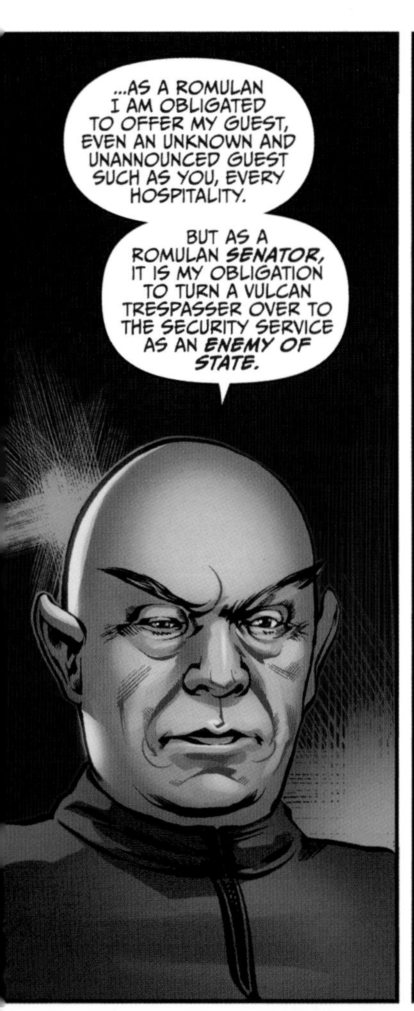
...AS A ROMULAN I AM OBLIGATED TO OFFER MY GUEST, EVEN AN UNKNOWN AND UNANNOUNCED GUEST SUCH AS YOU, EVERY HOSPITALITY.
BUT AS A ROMULAN **SENATOR**, IT IS MY OBLIGATION TO TURN A VULCAN TRESPASSER OVER TO THE SECURITY SERVICE AS AN **ENEMY OF STATE.**

TELL ME WHY I SHOULD NOT.
BECAUSE THE FUTURE OF **BOTH** OUR PEOPLES DEPENDS ON IT, SENATOR PARDEK.

YOU STILL HAVEN'T EXPLAINED HOW YOU KNOW MY NAME. **OR** WHERE I LIVE.
YOU WOULD NOT BELIEVE THE EXPLANATION.
BUT THE EXPLANATION IS ALL I HAVE TO OFFER.

AFTER I TELL YOU THE TRUTH OF MY CIRCUMSTANCES, YOU MAY DO AS YOU WISH.
VERY WELL.

I WAS NOT INCLINED TO SHARE THESE FACTS WITH *ANYONE*, BUT CIRCUMSTANCES HAVE DICTATED THAT I MUST.
YOU ARE THE ONLY ONE WITH WHOM I CAN AND WILL SHARE THIS INFORMATION.

I AM THE SOLE SURVIVOR OF AN ALTERNATE REALITY, FROM A TIME OVER A CENTURY LATER THAN THE ONE IN WHICH WE FIND OURSELVES NOW.
IN MY TIMELINE, ROMULUS WAS DESTROYED BY THE BLAST WAVE FROM A SUPERNOVA UNLIKE ANY ENCOUNTERED BEFORE.

NO DOUBT WORD HAS REACHED YOU OF *NERO*, THE ROMULAN WHO ENSURED THE DESTRUCTION OF VULCAN IN *THIS* REALITY.
MY PEOPLE NOW SEEK A NEW HOMEWORLD, BUT I HAVE BEEN EXILED FROM THEIR POPULATION.
IF I CANNOT CONVINCE YOU TO HELP ME, I FEAR THAT BOTH VULCANS *AND* ROMULANS ARE DOOMED TO EXTINCTION.
YOU.
YOU'RE THE ONE THE TATTOOED SURVIVORS SPOKE OF.
THE OLD VULCAN.

SURVIVORS?
NERO'S SHIP WAS DESTROYED, TOGETHER WITH ITS CREW.

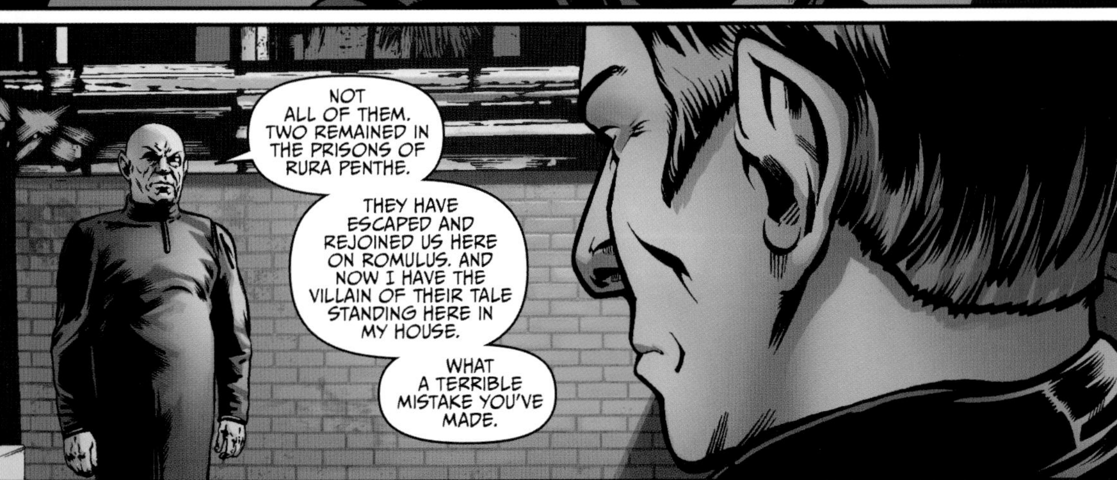
NOT ALL OF THEM. TWO REMAINED IN THE PRISONS OF RURA PENTHE.
THEY HAVE ESCAPED AND REJOINED US HERE ON ROMULUS. AND NOW I HAVE THE VILLAIN OF THEIR TALE STANDING HERE IN MY HOUSE.
WHAT A TERRIBLE MISTAKE YOU'VE MADE.

HAVE I?
OR IS MY LAST RESORT TO APPEAL TO THE FOUNDER OF THE ***ROMULAN RESISTANCE*** FOR HELP?

RESISTANCE--
--HOW--
--HOW COULD YOU ***POSSIBLY*** KNOW THAT?!

BECAUSE I KNOW...
...OR I SHOULD SAY *KNEW*...
...YOUR *SON*.

EXPLAIN YOURSELF!
IN MY TIME, YOUR SON FOLLOWED IN YOUR FOOTSTEPS, NOT ONLY BY BECOMING A SENATOR, BUT ALSO BY PURSUING *PEACE* BETWEEN OUR PEOPLES.

THIS--
THIS IS *IMPOSSIBLE*--
NO MORE IMPOSSIBLE THAN MY EXISTENCE HERE BEFORE YOU.

YOU ARE BOTH UNDER ARREST!

SENATOR PARDEK, YOU ARE HARBORING AN *ENEMY OF ROMULUS!*
BY THE POWERS OF THE PRAETOR AND SENATE, YOU ARE HEREBY STRIPPED OF ALL OFFICIAL CAPACITY AND ARE REMANDED TO THE CUSTODY OF THE SECURITY SERVICES!

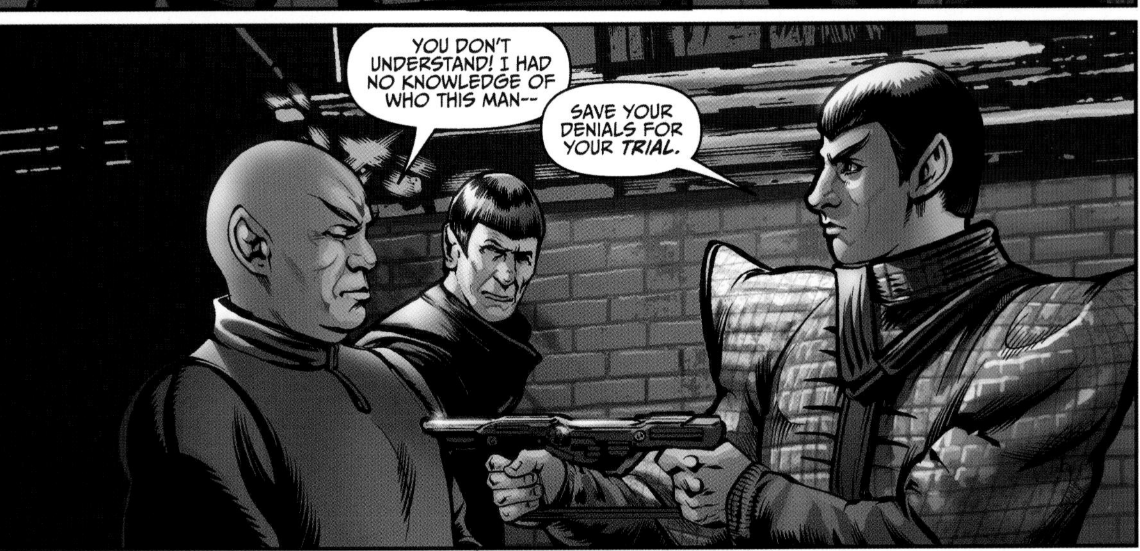
YOU DON'T UNDERSTAND! I HAD NO KNOWLEDGE OF WHO THIS MAN--
SAVE YOUR DENIALS FOR YOUR *TRIAL.*

AND *YOU*, YOU DECREPIT VULCAN, DID YOU REALLY THINK YOU COULD ARRIVE UNDETECTED?
I HOPE YOUR GAMBLE WAS WORTH IT...

"...BECAUSE YOU'RE NEVER LEAVING THIS PLANET AGAIN."
PRISONER!
YOU HAVE VISITORS!
IT REALLY IS YOU.

WE'RE SO HAPPY TO SEE YOU AGAIN, AMBASSADOR.

AN ALTERNATE TIMELINE.
THE 24TH CENTURY.
THE PLANET ROMULUS.

MY PREVIOUS STAY ON ROMULUS INCLUDED A VISIT FROM MOST *UNLIKELY* GUESTS. *
*AS SEEN IN EPISODE "UNIFICATION II" OF STAR TREK: THE NEXT GENERATION!

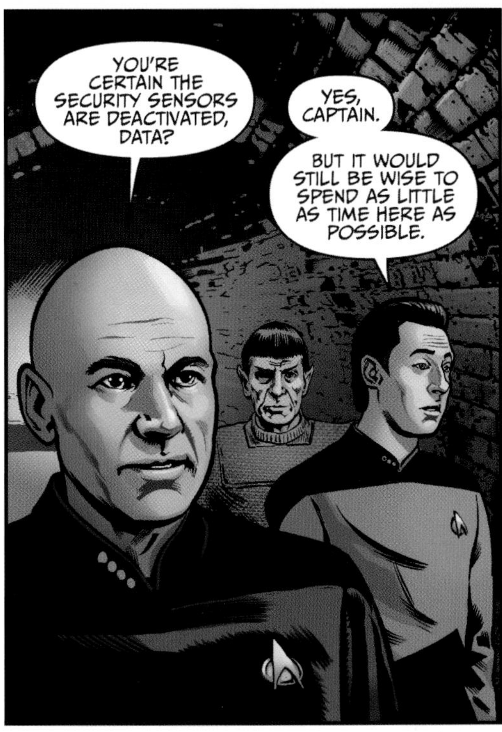
YOU'RE CERTAIN THE SECURITY SENSORS ARE DEACTIVATED, DATA?
YES, CAPTAIN.
BUT IT WOULD STILL BE WISE TO SPEND AS LITTLE AS TIME HERE AS POSSIBLE.

WAIT...
REET REET REET REET

A SECURITY DRONE. I COULD NOT SHUT THEM DOWN REMOTELY. WE MUST BE ALERT.
ONCE WE ARE FREE OF THE *CAPITOL PERIMETER* OUR PATH WILL BE LESS HAZARDOUS.

THROUGH HERE, QUICKLY.
THE SECURITY GRID MAY REACTIVATE AT ANY TIME.

I MUST SAY I'M IMPRESSED, SPOCK.
MOST AMBASSADORS YOUR AGE ARE ENJOYING A WELL-EARNED *RETIREMENT* ABOARD A WELL-APPOINTED *LEISURE CRAFT.*

AND MOST *CAPTAINS* PREFER TO CARRY OUT THEIR ORDERS FROM THE BRIDGE OF A STARSHIP...
...NOT COLLABORATING WITH A *DISSIDENT POLITICAL MOVEMENT* ON THE GROUND.

OR *UNDER* IT.
BUT THIS WAS A MISSION I COULD NOT REFUSE.

NOT SO MUCH BECAUSE OF YOUR DUTY TO STARFLEET, I SENSE...
...BUT BECAUSE OF YOUR FRIENDSHIP WITH MY **FATHER.**

INDEED.
SAREK AND I SHARED A SPECIAL BOND.
BUT THE TRUTH IS THAT YOU HAVE OPENED MY EYES--OPENED **STARFLEET'S** EYES--TO SOMETHING **NEW.**

I FEAR WE TOO OFTEN RESIGN OURSELVES TO THE INEVITABILITY OF **CONFLICT** BETWEEN THE FEDERATION AND ROMULUS.
YOUR WORK HERE REMINDS ME THAT **PEACE IS POSSIBLE.**

I BELIEVE PEACE IS SIMPLY **LOGICAL.**
THE EVIDENCE FOR THAT BELIEF...

...STANDS BEFORE YOU NOW. ROMULANS WHO BELIEVE THAT WAR IS *NOT* INEVITABLE.
THEY REPRESENT THE *FUTURE.*

MY BELIEF PROVED CORRECT.
IN THE DECADES TO COME, THE PEACEFUL OVERTURES BETWEEN ROMULANS AND VULCANS WOULD GROW TO SUCH AN EXTENT THAT I COULD WORK *OPENLY* AS AN AMBASSADOR HERE.
UNTIL THE TRAGEDY.
ROMULUS WAS DESTROYED.
VULCAN WAS BLAMED...

AND I NOW FIND MYSELF BACK ON ROMULUS, WITH ALL MY WORK UNDONE.
A NEW TIMELINE.
ONE CENTURY PRIOR.
SPOCK OF VULCAN.
YOU STAND ACCUSED.
THESE TWO BRAVE ROMULANS--
--SURVIVORS OF OUR PLANET'S DESTRUCTION IN THEIR ORIGINAL TIME--
--HAVE SUPPLIED THIS SENATE WITH ALL THE TESTIMONY IT REQUIRES TO KNOW THE TRUTH.

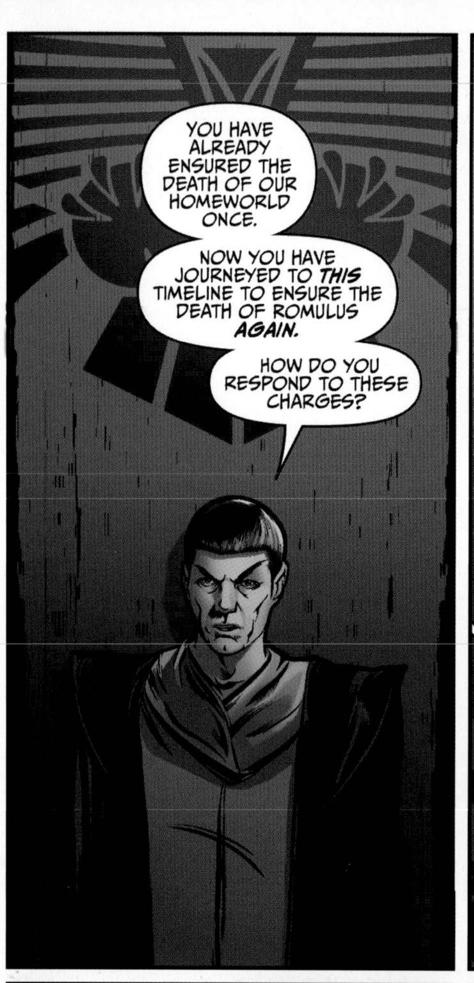

YOU HAVE ALREADY ENSURED THE DEATH OF OUR HOMEWORLD ONCE.
NOW YOU HAVE JOURNEYED TO *THIS* TIMELINE TO ENSURE THE DEATH OF ROMULUS *AGAIN.*
HOW DO YOU RESPOND TO THESE CHARGES?

A *SMILE?*

YOU MAKE A *MOCKERY* OF THESE PROCEEDINGS, VULCAN!

NO MOCKERY IS INTENDED, PRAETOR.
I AM SIMPLY STRUCK BY THE *IRONY* OF MY SITUATION.
IN THE EYES OF THE ROMULAN SENATE, I AM A VULCAN.
BUT TO MY OWN PEOPLE, THE LAST SURVIVORS OF *OUR* HOMEWORLD'S DESTRUCTION...
...I AM NOT.

THEY HAVE *EXILED* ME.
THEY HAVE-- ***LOGICALLY,*** IN THEIR MINDS--FOUND ME CULPABLE IN PART FOR OUR PLANET'S DESTRUCTION DUE TO MY INABILITY TO PREVENT THE TERRORIST NERO FROM ARRIVING IN THIS TIMELINE.

I CANNOT SAY WITH ANY CERTAINTY THAT THEIR CONCLUSIONS ARE INCORRECT.
ALL I CAN DO NOW IS TO PREVENT ***FURTHER*** TRAGEDY, BY DOING WHATEVER I CAN TO FOSTER ***PEACE*** BETWEEN OUR PEOPLES.

FALSEHOODS!
YOU ***CLAIM*** TO BE EXILED, WHEN IN FACT YOU TRAVELED HERE TO ROMULUS--***VIOLATING*** OUR IMPERIAL BORDERS--ON THE ORDERS OF THE VULCAN ELDERS!

FOR ALL OF THE VULCANS' FAMOUS ***DISDAIN OF EMOTION,*** IT IS OBVIOUS THAT YOU ARE HERE ON A MISSION OF ***PURE REVENGE.***

QUITE THE OPPOSITE.
I WISH FOR THOSE IN A POSITION TO CHANGE THE FUTURE OF ROMULUS TO KNOW OF THE **DANGER** THAT WAITS FOR YOU IN THIS TIMELINE.
THE **HOBUS STAR** IS UNSTABLE, AS IT WAS IN MY TIME. BUT YOU HAVE THE BENEFIT OF KNOWING **NOW** THAT ITS IMPENDING SUPERNOVA WILL DESTROY ROMULUS.
YOU CAN STILL TAKE ACTION TO SAVE YOUR PEOPLE.
HE LIES! VELLA AND I WERE **THERE!**
WE **SAW** HIM **TRICK** NERO INTO TRUSTING HIM!
NOW HE WANTS YOU TO **ABANDON** THE HOMEWORLD SO THAT THE SURVIVING VULCANS CAN CLAIM IT FOR **THEMSELVES!**
ENOUGH.
SPOCK OF VULCAN, IT IS THE JUDGMENT OF THIS BODY THAT YOU AND THE TRAITOROUS SENATOR PARDEK BE EXECUTED AS AN EXAMPLE TO ALL WHO WOULD SEEK TO UNDERMINE OUR PROUD EMPIRE.
YOU HAVE ONE LAST NIGHT TO PRAY TO WHATEVER FALSE GODS YOU WORSHIP...

"MAY THEY HAVE MERCY ON YOUR SOUL."

SENATOR PARDEK.
I WAS WRONG ABOUT YOU, SPOCK.
AND I MAY AS WELL CONFESS THAT YOU WERE QUITE RIGHT ABOUT ME.
NOW WE GO TO OUR FATES TOGETHER.

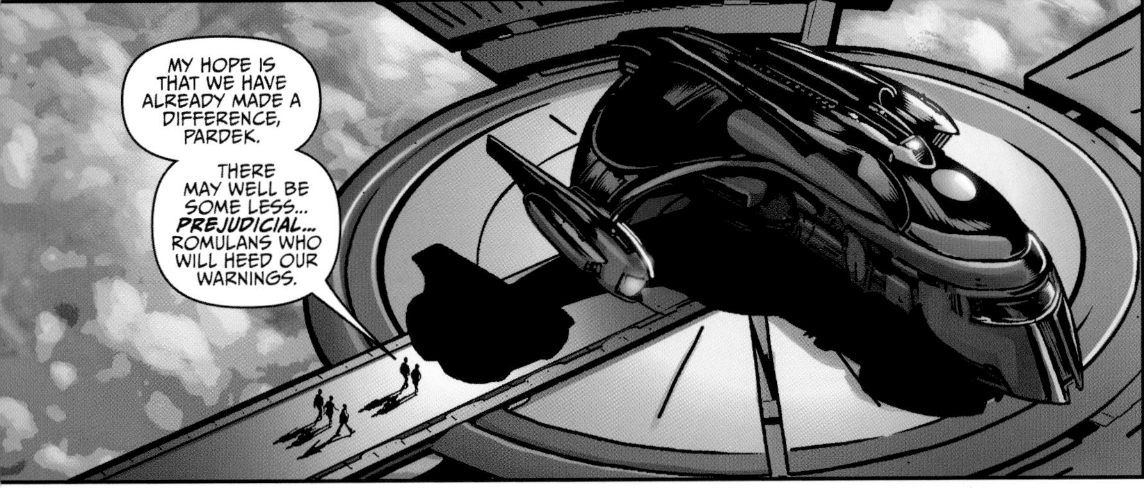
MY HOPE IS THAT WE HAVE ALREADY MADE A DIFFERENCE, PARDEK.
THERE MAY WELL BE SOME LESS... PREJUDICIAL... ROMULANS WHO WILL HEED OUR WARNINGS.

THERE MAY BE MORE OF THOSE OPEN-MINDED ROMULANS THAN YOU THINK, SPOCK.

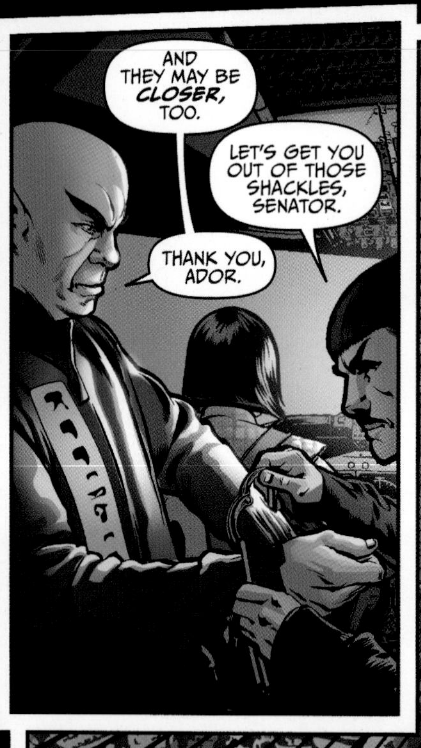
AND THEY MAY BE CLOSER, TOO.
LET'S GET YOU OUT OF THOSE SHACKLES, SENATOR.
THANK YOU, ADOR.

SECURITY SHUTTLE AVEM-4, YOU ARE NOT CLEARED FOR DEPARTURE.
RETURN IMMEDIATELY.

AVEM-4, THIS IS YOUR FINAL WARNING!
DAMN. I THOUGHT WE'D HAVE A LITTLE MORE TIME BEFORE THEY NOTICED.

I UNDERESTIMATED THE STRENGTH OF YOUR RESISTANCE MOVEMENT, PARDEK.
IT IS MORE EXTENSIVE IN THIS TIME PERIOD THAN I GUESSED IT TO BE.

EVERYTHING CHANGED AFTER VULCAN'S DESTRUCTION, SPOCK.
BUT YOUR ARRIVAL HERE HAS EMBOLDENED US.

AVEM-4, YOU ARE TRANSPORTING IMPERIAL PRISONERS WITHOUT AUTHORIZATION!
RETURN AT ONCE OR WE WILL SHOOT YOU DOWN!
ADOR, ARE YOU SURE YOU SABOTAGED **ALL** THE PATROL SHIPS ON STANDBY?
AND DISABLED THE DETECTION GRIDS OVER THE SECTORS WE'RE ENTERING?
TRUST ME **FOR ONCE,** BELIA...
BAANG
BAANG
...WHAT'S THE USE OF A **BREAKOUT** IF THERE'S NO **GETAWAY?**

ONE HOUR LATER.
DON'T HATE ME!

I NEVER INTENDED TO TURN YOU OVER TO THE AUTHORITIES!
IT WAS ALL I COULD DO TO TALK MY WAY OUT OF THEIR CUSTODY AND AVOID MY OWN EXECUTION FOR UNAPPROVED ENTRY INTO ROMULAN SPACE!

AND HOW MUCH IS THE RESISTANCE PAYING YOU TO FLY ME OFF ROMULUS?

NEVER MIND THAT. I ALREADY SPENT MOST OF IT ON A NEW CLOAKING DEVICE TO GET US OUT OF HERE.
BELIEVE IT OR NOT, I HAVE DECIDED TO JOIN SENATOR PARDEK'S CAUSE!

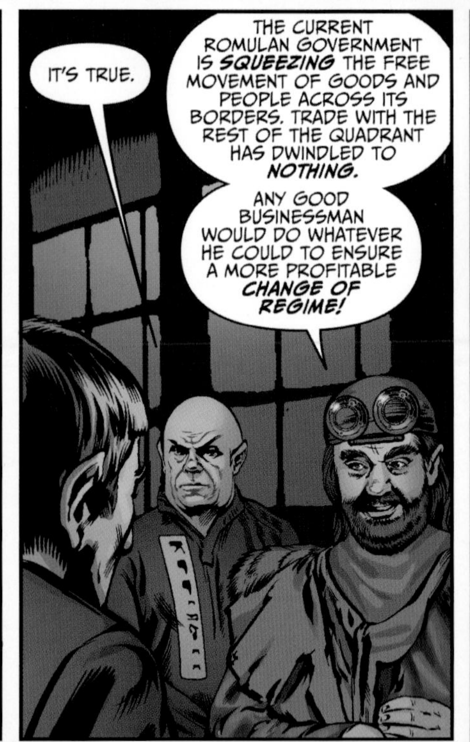
IT'S TRUE.
THE CURRENT ROMULAN GOVERNMENT IS SQUEEZING THE FREE MOVEMENT OF GOODS AND PEOPLE ACROSS ITS BORDERS. TRADE WITH THE REST OF THE QUADRANT HAS DWINDLED TO NOTHING.
ANY GOOD BUSINESSMAN WOULD DO WHATEVER HE COULD TO ENSURE A MORE PROFITABLE CHANGE OF REGIME!

ARE YOU SURE YOU WILL BE SAFE REMAINING HERE ON ROMULUS, SENATOR?
HARDLY. BUT IT IS CRUCIAL THAT I DO.
AS FOR YOU, SPOCK, WHEN YOU RETURN TO THE OTHER VULCANS...
...WHAT MAKES YOU BELIEVE THAT THEY WILL LISTEN TO YOU?
MY WORDS, MORE THAN MY PRESENCE.
THE ELDERS CANNOT AFFORD TO IGNORE YOUR SPIES' REPORTS OF THE LAST REMNANTS OF RED MATTER IN ROMULAN HANDS, AND THEIR INTENT TO ATTACK THE VULCAN FLEET.
LIVE LONG AND PROSPER, PARDEK.
JOLAN TRU, SPOCK...

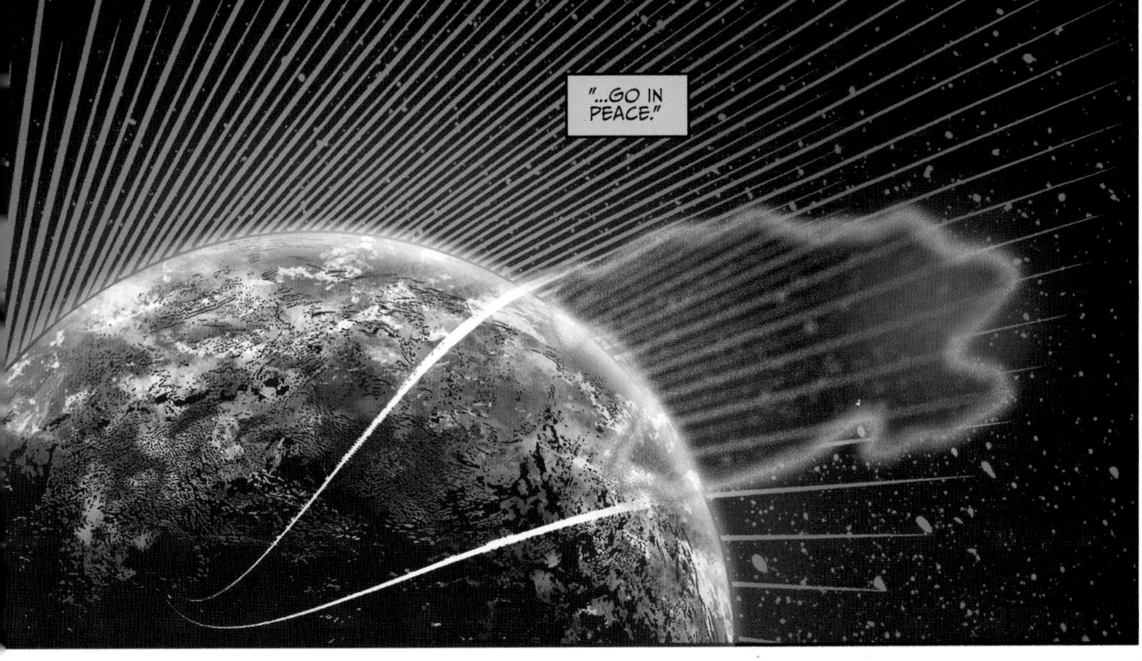
"...GO IN PEACE."

"WHAT WAS IT YOU WISHED TO DISCUSS, SAREK?"
IF IT IS SPOCK'S WARNING REGARDING OUR PLAN TO COLONIZE CETI ALPHA V, I CAN ASSURE YOU THAT OUR SCIENTISTS HAVE CONDUCTED EXTENSIVE TESTS OF THE PLANET AND ITS SYSTEM.
THEY ARE CONVINCED OF ITS *SUITABILITY.*
I DID NOT WISH TO SPEAK OF *THAT* WARNING, ELDER T'PAH. ALTHOUGH HE WAS QUITE CONVINCED OF ITS VERACITY.
I SPEAK OF A *NEW* ONE HE HAS DELIVERED TO ME WHILE EN ROUTE FROM ROMULUS.
YOU HAVE BEEN *COMMUNICATING* WITH SPOCK?
AND HE HAS VISITED *ROMULUS?*

HE WAS DOING WHAT HE THOUGHT BEST TO ENSURE THE SAFETY OF ALL VULCANS.
EVEN **AFTER** HE WAS EXILED FROM THEM.

YOUR INSTINCT TO TRUST SPOCK IS UNDERSTANDABLE, SAREK, GIVEN YOUR.... ***UNIQUE...***RELATIONSHIP WITH HIM.

BUT HE SPENT AN ENTIRE ***LIFETIME*** IN ANOTHER REALITY, ABOUT WHICH WE KNOW ***ONLY*** WHAT HE HAS TOLD US.

WHAT IF HE ACQUIRED ROMULAN ***SYMPATHIES*** OVER THE COURSE OF HIS LIFE?

THEN I DOUBT THE TERRORIST NERO WOULD HAVE BEEN SO EAGER TO SEE HIS DEMISE.

I ASK ONLY THAT YOU LISTEN TO HIM. IF NOT FOR MY SAKE, OR HIS...

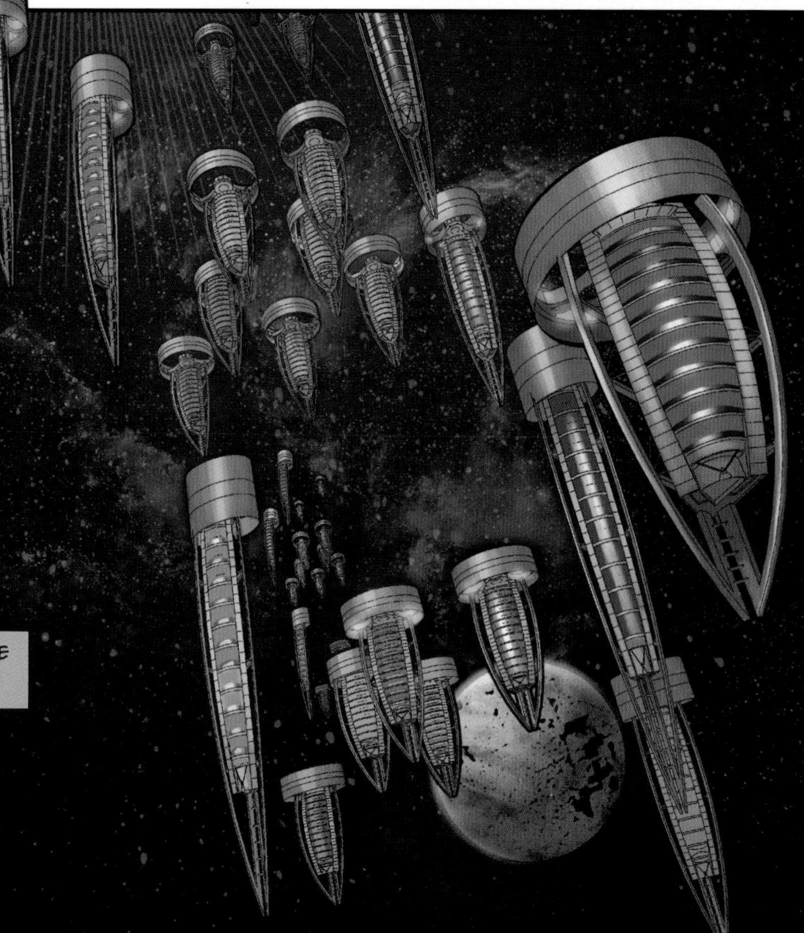

"...THEN FOR THE SAKE OF OUR PEOPLE."

HOW THE HELL COULD YOU LET HIM ESCAPE?!
PROUD SON OF ROMULUS OR NOT, YOU WOULD BE WISE TO WATCH YOUR TONE WHEN ADDRESSING A **SENATOR!**
NOT TO MENTION ACCUSING THEM OF ***INCOMPETENCE!***

SPOCK HAD AN UNFORESEEN ALLY IN SENATOR PARDEK. WE WERE ***BETRAYED*** BY ONE OF OUR OWN.

FORGIVE ARIX, SENATORS.
OUR JOURNEY HAS BEEN A LONG ONE. TO HAVE OUR REVENGE ON SPOCK RIPPED FROM OUR GRASP JUST WHEN IT WAS SO CLOSE...

YOU WILL HAVE IT, AND SOONER THAN YOU THINK.
PARDEK KNEW OF OUR PLAN TO USE THE REMAINING RED MATTER TO DESTROY THE VULCAN SURVIVORS.
SPOCK WILL BE ON HIS WAY TO WARN THEM.

IT WILL BE TOO LATE. THE VANGUARD OF OUR FLEET WILL BE CLOSE BEHIND.
HIS ARRIVAL HERE CONVINCED THE REST OF THE SENATE THAT THE WISEST COURSE OF ACTION IS TO ATTACK THE VULCANS WHILE THEY ARE AT THEIR WEAKEST.

THERE IS NOT ENOUGH OF THE RED ELEMENT LEFT TO DESTROY A PLANET, BUT THERE IS ENOUGH TO DESTROY THE ASSEMBLED VULCAN FLEET.
IT CANNOT BE DONE REMOTELY. A BRAVE PILOT--

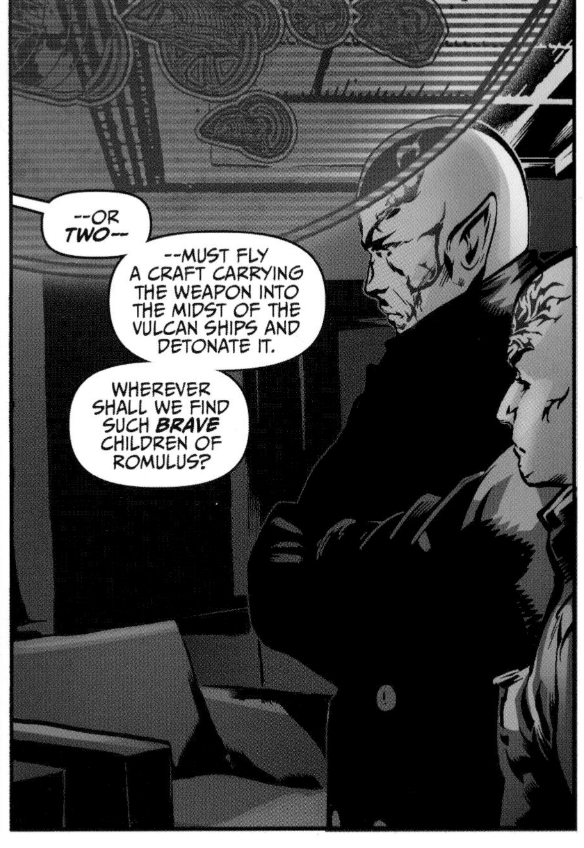
--OR ***TWO***--
--MUST FLY A CRAFT CARRYING THE WEAPON INTO THE MIDST OF THE VULCAN SHIPS AND DETONATE IT.
WHEREVER SHALL WE FIND SUCH ***BRAVE*** CHILDREN OF ROMULUS?

"THANK YOU FOR AGREEING TO SEE ME, ELDER T'PAH."
DO NOT TAKE IT TO MEAN THAT YOUR EXILE IS OVER, SPOCK.
BUT IT WOULD NOT BE LOGICAL TO AT LEAST CONSIDER ADDITIONAL INFORMATION YOU HAVE OBTAINED REGARDING ROMULAN INTENTIONS TOWARD US.
AND SAREK HAS BEEN A TRUSTED CONFIDANT FOR TOO LONG SIMPLY TO IGNORE HIS COUNSEL NOW.
YOU SAY THE ROMULANS ARE PLANNING AN ATTACK ON OUR FLEET?

NOT SIMPLY "AN" ATTACK, ELDER T'PAH.
A *FINAL* ONE. AND SOON.

THEN WE MAKE OUR STAND *HERE,* AT CETI ALPHA V.
TO FLEE NOW WOULD ONLY INVITE FURTHER PURSUIT. AN ENDLESS CHASE THAT COULD ONLY DEPLETE OUR ALREADY LIMITED RESOURCES.

WE SHOULD SEND WORD TO STARFLEET. THEY WILL COME TO OUR DEFENSE.
ASSUMING, OF COURSE, THAT THEY REACH US BEFORE THE ROMULANS DO.

THERE IS LOGIC IN CHOOSING TO STAND AND FIGHT.
BUT KNOW THIS...

"THE ROMULANS WILL SEND EVERY SHIP...
"THEY WILL SEND EVERY SOLDIER...
"THEY WILL SEND EVERY WEAPON THEY HAVE...
"...UNTIL THE LAST VULCAN IS DEAD."

IT HAS ALL COME DOWN TO THIS.
WAR IN ORBIT OVER CETI ALPHA V.
THE ROMULAN EMPIRE HAS SENT THEIR FLEET TO ELIMINATE THE LAST SURVIVING VULCANS, WHO SEEK TO BUILD A NEW HOME ON THIS WORLD.
I ARRIVED JUST IN TIME TO WARN MY PEOPLE OF THE THREAT.

BUT AS I WATCH THE FLASHES OF LIGHT IN THE SKY ABOVE, I CAN ONLY WONDER IF OUR TRUE ENEMY...
...IS A *DESTINY* WE CANNOT HOPE TO ESCAPE.

SPOCK.
WE ARE MONITORING THE BATTLE FROM INSIDE THE CAMP. YOU ARE WELCOME TO JOIN US.

THE ELDERS' REFUSAL TO ASK FOR STARFLEET'S HELP IS ILLOGICAL. OUR SHIPS ARE OUTMATCHED, SAREK.
THE ELDERS BELIEVE THAT STARFLEET FAILED US ALREADY, WHEN OUR PLANET WAS DESTROYED.
THEY BELIEVE THAT IT IS OUR RESPONSIBILITY TO ENSURE *OUR OWN* SURVIVAL NOW.

A DISTURBINGLY *EMOTIONAL* REACTION.
BUT EVEN WITH STARFLEET'S HELP, THE ROMULANS STILL POSSESS A WEAPON WHOSE POWER IS UNMATCHED...

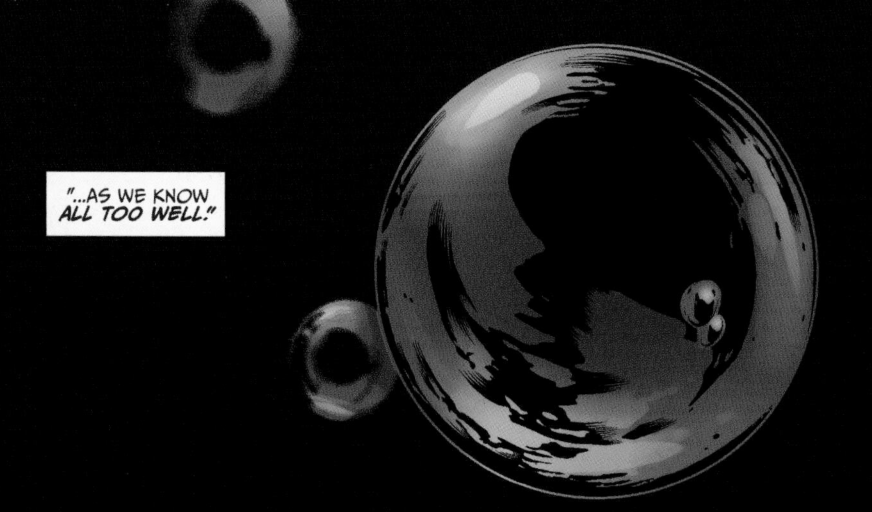
"...AS WE KNOW ALL TOO WELL."

THE PAYLOAD WILL SOON BE READY.
ALL THAT REMAINS IS TO DELIVER THE LAST DROP OF RED MATTER IN EXISTENCE INTO THE HEART OF THE VULCAN FLEET.
AFTER THAT IT WILL BE EASY ENOUGH TO PICK OFF ANY REMAINING SHIPS, AND WIPE OUT ANY SURVIVORS ON THE PLANET'S SURFACE.

RELLA...WE HAVE JOURNEYED FAR TOGETHER. BUT ONLY ONE OF US NEEDS TO PILOT THE SHIP UNTIL DETONATION.
LEAVE ME TO DO IT.

LEAVE YOU? AND GO WHERE? WE ARE STRANGERS IN THIS NEW REALITY.
EVERYONE WE EVER KNEW IS DEAD. OUR WIVES, OUR CHILDREN, OUR PARENTS, OUR FRIENDS.
DEAD.

MY PLACE--MY HOME--IS WITH YOU, NOW.

WE ARE LOSING THIS BATTLE.
"THE ROMULAN FLEET IS SIMPLY TOO POWERFUL.
"IT IS DESIGNED TO OVERWHELM A FLEET LIKE OURS, WHICH IS INTENDED ONLY FOR EXPLORATION AND DEFENSE."
AT THIS RATE THEY WILL HAVE NO NEED TO USE THEIR RED MATTER AT ALL!
THE LOGICAL COURSE OF ACTION IS TO ENSURE THE SURVIVAL OF OUR HERITAGE AND EVACUATE THE ELDERS AT ONCE!

ABANDON THE REST OF OUR PEOPLE?
YOUR **FEAR** OF LOSING YOUR **OWN** LIFE IS ***UNBECOMING*** OF YOUR STATION.

ELDER T'PAH! WE HAVE DETECTED A NEW SHIP IN ORBIT!
THEY ARE HAILING US!
--ZZKKT--ULCAN COMMAND, THIS IS--ZZTK

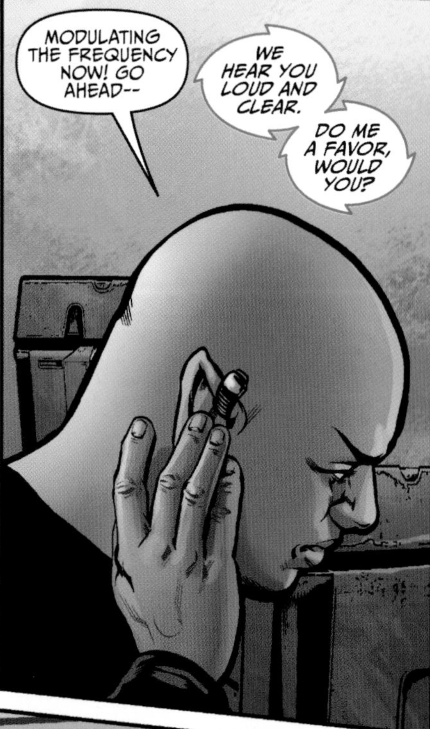
MODULATING THE FREQUENCY NOW! GO AHEAD--
WE HEAR YOU LOUD AND CLEAR.
DO ME A FAVOR, WOULD YOU?

ASK AMBASSADOR SPOCK WHY HE LEFT WITHOUT SAYING ***GOODBYE.***
OH, AND TO USE AN OLD EARTH EXPRESSION--

"--THE CAVALRY'S HERE!"
CAPTAIN, WE DID NOT ISSUE A DISTRESS CALL.
YOU MUST NOT RISK YOUR SHIP ON OUR BEHALF.

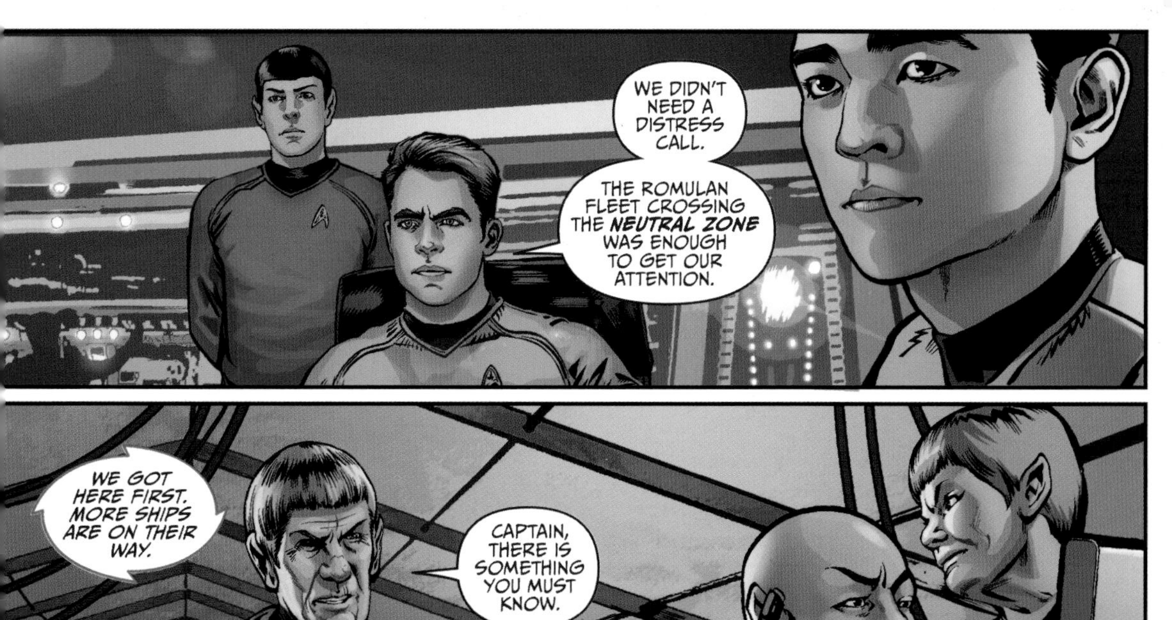
WE DIDN'T NEED A DISTRESS CALL.
THE ROMULAN FLEET CROSSING THE NEUTRAL ZONE WAS ENOUGH TO GET OUR ATTENTION.

WE GOT HERE FIRST. MORE SHIPS ARE ON THEIR WAY.
CAPTAIN, THERE IS SOMETHING YOU MUST KNOW.

I WAS ONLY JOKING ABOUT THE GOODBYE, AMBASSADOR. IT'S GOOD TO HEAR YOUR VOICE.
AND YOURS, CAPTAIN. BUT THERE IS A SINGLE ROMULAN SHIP CARRYING THE LAST REMAINING PARTICLE OF RED MATTER.
IT MUST BE DISABLED BEFORE IT DESTROYS US ALL.
UNDERSTOOD.

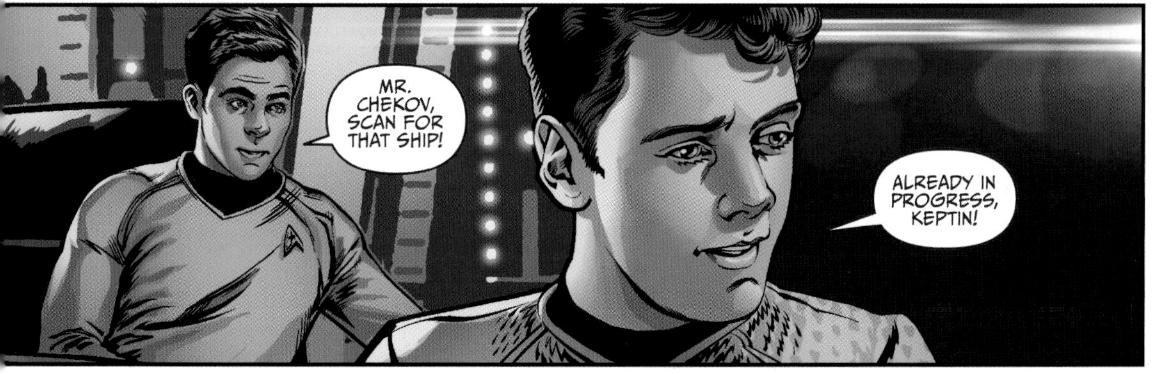
MR. CHEKOV, SCAN FOR THAT SHIP!
ALREADY IN PROGRESS, KEPTIN!

MORE STARFLEET SHIPS ARRIVING!

THE ENTERPRISE IS SCANNING US. WE MUST ACT NOW.
TO ALL ROMULAN SHIPS: DISENGAGE! WE ARE BEGINNING THE DETONATION COUNTDOWN!

"GET CLEAR OF THE BLAST ZONE!"

KEPTIN, THE ROMULAN FLEET IS RETREATING--

"EXCEPT FOR ONE SHIP!"

CAPTAIN--
I KNOW, COMMANDER.
THAT'S THE SHIP WE'RE AFTER.

"TARGET PHOTON TORPEDOES, MR. SULU!"
"AYE SIR!"

AT LAST, OUR WORK IS DONE.
THE TREACHERY OF THE VULCAN RACE WILL NO LONGER--

FORGIVE ME, RELLA.

CAPTAIN, THE TARGET--
--IT'S *RETREATING!*
KEEP WEAPONS LOCKED ON, SULU. WE CAN'T LET THEM LEAVE WITH THAT CARGO.
CAPTAIN, THEY'RE HAILING US!
WE ARE BEING HAILED BY THE ROMULAN SHIP.
OPENING A CHANNEL.

IF YOU CAN HEAR THIS, YOU ARE MY ENEMY.

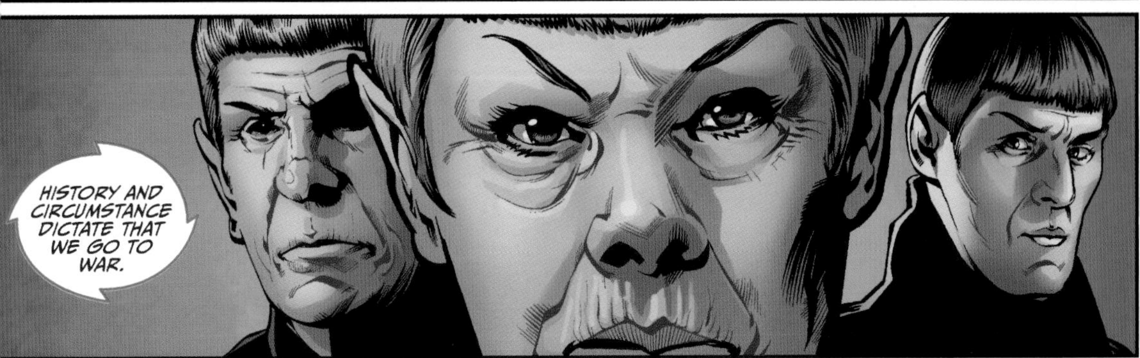
HISTORY AND CIRCUMSTANCE DICTATE THAT WE GO TO WAR.

...BUT I AM NOT A WARRIOR.
I JUST AM A SIMPLE MINER. I HAD A FAMILY. I HAD A HOME.

I NEVER WANTED ANYTHING MORE.
FATE CHOSE OTHERWISE FOR ME.

AND NOW I AM HERE, CARRYING A WEAPON MEANT TO ENSURE EVEN MORE DEATH THAN I HAVE ALREADY WITNESSED...
AND MY CHOICE IS CLEAR TO ME.

FIRE ON ME IF YOU MUST, CAPTAIN.
BUT THE RESULT WILL BE THE SAME.

THERE WILL BE NO MORE TRAGEDY TODAY.

...LET HIM GO, MR. SULU. MAINTAIN SAFE DISTANCE.
AYE, SIR.

THEY ARE ALLOWING HIM TO ESCAPE?
NO. NOT TO ESCAPE.

"TO SEEK REDEMPTION."

"THE ROMULANS THOUGHT THEY COULD CATCH STARFLEET SLEEPING."

THEY WON'T RISK ANOTHER ATTACK ON YOU NOW THAT THEY KNOW THE FEDERATION WILL RESPOND.
YOUR ASSISTANCE WAS NOT REQUESTED, CAPTAIN KIRK...
...BUT IT IS MOST APPRECIATED. OUR COLONY HERE IS NOW FREE TO GROW IN PEACE.

YEAH, ABOUT THAT...
...YOU SHOULD REALLY LISTEN TO AMBASSADOR SPOCK'S ADVICE ABOUT CHOOSING A NEW LOCATION. CETI ALPHA V IS NO PLACE TO PUT DOWN ROOTS.

AND YOU KNOW THIS HOW?
WELL, WHEN I FIRST MET THE AMBASSADOR, WE, UH...I'M NOT SURE HOW TO PUT THIS, BUT HE...
I *MIND-MELDED* WITH THE CAPTAIN.

IN DOING SO, HE LEARNED OF THE EVENTS IN MY ORIGINAL TIMELINE.
HE SAW THAT CETI ALPHA V IS DOOMED.

WE SHOULD BELIEVE THE HUMAN WITHOUT ANY EVIDENCE TO SUPPORT THIS CLAIM?
AND I SHOULD REMIND YOU, SPOCK, THAT YOUR STATUS WITHIN OUR COMMUNITY IS STILL IN QUESTION.

THERE IS A SIMPLE WAY TO PROVE BOTH MY VERACITY **AND** MY LOYALTY.
OPEN YOUR MIND TO ME, AND ALLOW THE OTHER ELDERS TO DO THE SAME.

A MIND-MELD?
IT WOULD PROVIDE YOU WITH THE EVIDENCE YOU SEEK.

...VERY WELL.
COME, LET US DISCOVER THE TRUTH TOGETHER.
IT REMAINS MY WISH NOT TO INTERFERE IN THIS NEW TIMELINE ANY MORE THAN IS NECESSARY.
AND SO I OPEN MY MIND...

...I SHOW THEM JUST ENOUGH.

ONE YEAR LATER.
THE SECOND PLANET OF SYSTEM SIMON-316.

WE FOUNDED THE NEW VULCAN COLONY ON AN UNINHABITED WORLD.
MOSTLY UNINHABITED.
WHILE ONLY HALF THE SIZE OF VULCAN, THIS NEW PLANET'S CLIMATE AND TOPOGRAPHY IS REMARKABLY SIMILAR.
IT FEELS, AS AN ORNERY DOCTOR I ONCE KNEW MIGHT SAY...

...JUST LIKE HOME.

THE LAST HOME I WILL KNOW IN THIS LIFE.
THE TIME GROWS NEAR.

BUT I KNOW THAT THE FUTURE OF MY PEOPLE IS SECURE.

ITS POPULATION GROWING.

ITS PLACE WITHIN THE FEDERATION ASSURED.

AS FOR MYSELF, I HAVE BEEN BLESSED WITH A LONG LIFE.
AND, BY EVERY MEASURE THAT TRULY MATTERS...

...A MOST PROSPEROUS ONE.

NEW VULCAN.
THREE THOUSAND YEARS LATER.
WHY HAVE WE COME ALL THIS WAY, FATHER?
THERE IS SOMETHING I WISH FOR YOU TO SEE.
WHO IS THAT, FATHER?
THAT IS SPOCK.
ONE OF THE GREATEST OF ALL VULCANS.

In memory of Leonard Nimoy 1931 - 2015

U.S.S. ENTERPRISE
NCC – 1701
Cover by J

CONNECTION

Cover by Tony Shasteen

CAPTAIN'S LOG, SUPPLEMENTAL.
REET
REET
REET
I WOKE UP IN A STRANGER'S ROOM.
AT FIRST I THOUGHT IT WAS A DREAM.

CAPTAIN'S LOG, SUPPLEMENTAL.
BEEBEEP
BEEBEEP
BEEBEEP
I WOKE UP IN A PLACE I DIDN'T RECOGNIZE.
I THOUGHT IT WAS A DREAM AT FIRST.

THE UNIFORM FIT PERFECTLY, BUT THE COLOR AND DETAILS WERE OFF.

THAT WAS JUST THE START OF THE SURPRISES.
GOOD MORNING, CAPTAIN!

THE TAILORING WAS PERFECT, BUT THE COLOR AND DETAILS WERE...
UNUSUAL.

THE UNIFORM WOULD PROVE TO BE THE LEAST OF THE SURPRISES.
GOOD MORNING, CAPTAIN!

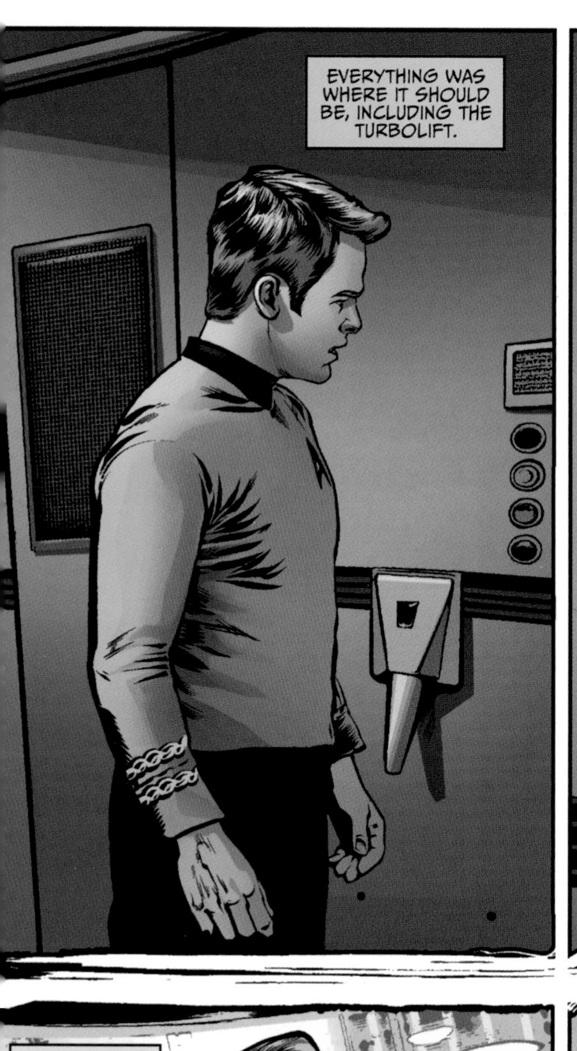
EVERYTHING WAS WHERE IT SHOULD BE, INCLUDING THE TURBOLIFT.

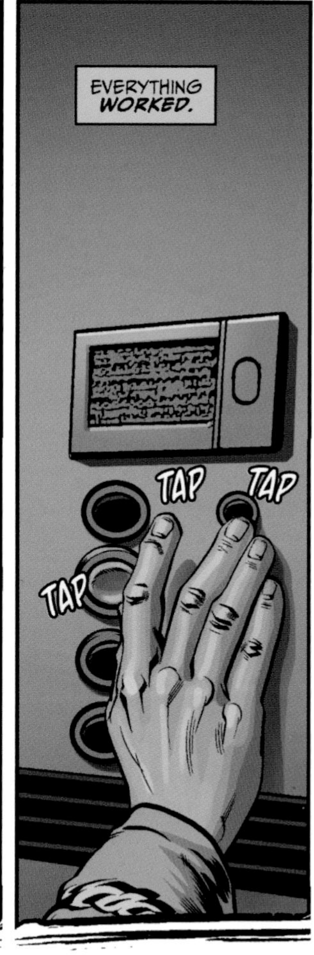
EVERYTHING *WORKED.*
TAP
TAP
TAP

WITH EVERY STEP I TOOK, I BECAME MORE CONVINCED...

CORRIDORS, TURBOLIFTS...

...EVEN THE CONTROL PADS WERE IN THE RIGHT PLACE.
TAP
TAP
TAP

WITH EVERY MOMENT THAT PASSED, IT BECAME CLEAR...

...THAT THIS WAS NO DREAM.
WE HAVE ENCOUNTERED A MOST UNUSUAL ANOMALY, CAPTAIN.
...THAT THIS WAS NO DREAM.
CAPTAIN, OUR SCANS INDICATE THAT WE HAVE FOUND A REGION OF SPACE UNLIKE ANY WE HAVE SEEN BEFORE.

IT'S HIM! THE OLDER SPOCK! BUT NOW HE'S...
IS SOMETHING WRONG, CAPTAIN?
...WHAT IS THIS?

WHERE AM I?
BRIDGE TO DR. MCCOY. PLEASE REPORT TO THE BRIDGE.

...WHERE IS SPOCK?
I AM RIGHT HERE, CAPTAIN. ARE YOU ALL RIGHT?

NO...NO, I DON'T THINK I AM...
BRIDGE TO SICKBAY.
DR. MCCOY, YOUR PRESENCE IS REQUIRED ON THE BRIDGE.

WAIT. WHO--
CAPTAIN, IT'S ME. IT'S LIEUTENANT UHURA!
--IS THAT?!
WAIT. THAT FACE--
CAPTAIN, MAYBE YOU SHOULD SIT DOWN...
WARP PLASMA 01
COMM BOX
0.2 0.3 0.4 0.5 0.6 0.7 0.8 0.9
--THAT'S NOT ME!

Q'S COME BACK TO MESS WITH US AGAIN...
WHO IS "Q," KEPTIN?

UNNH
FSSSH

CHANGING REALITY... THIS MUST BE TRELANE'S DOING...
WHO IS "TRELANE," KEPTIN?

HHNN
KTSSH

YOU HAVE THE CONN, MR. SPOCK.
KEEP ME APPRISED OF THE CAPTAIN'S CONDITION, DOCTOR.
LET'S GET YOU TO SICKBAY, JIM...
...AND FIND OUT WHAT CROSSED YOUR WIRES.
SEDATING THE CAPTAIN SEEMS EXTREME IN THIS CASE, DOCTOR.
DO ME A FAVOR, COMMANDER...
...AND LEAVE THE MEDICAL DECISIONS TO THE PROFESSIONALS.

RELAX, BONES.
I'VE EXPERIENCED PLENTY OF STRANGER THINGS BEFORE!
HOW *REASSURING.* SIT STILL.
YOUR DESCRIPTION OF THE EVENT IS MOST CURIOUS, CAPTAIN.
YOU SAY THAT EACH OF US, AND THE SHIP ITSELF, APPEARED COMPLETELY DIFFERENT?

STOP FIDGETING. IT MESSES UP THE SCAN.
IT WAS THE *ENTERPRISE*... ONLY...*NOT.*

EVERYTHING WAS BRIGHTER. THE LIGHTS FLARED.
AND THERE WERE...PANES OF GLASS JUST...STANDING THERE ON THE BRIDGE.
YOU...OR RATHER, THE OTHER SPOCK... SPOKE OF AN ANOMALY?
INDEED, CAPTAIN. WE HAVE DISCOVERED A REGION OF SPACE WITH MOST UNUSUAL PROPERTIES.
WE ARE DETECTING A LOCALIZED FLUCTUATION IN SPACE-TIME.
I'M NO PHYSICIST, BUT I DOUBT IT'S A COINCIDENCE THAT WE FOUND IT JUST WHEN THE CAPTAIN LOST HIS FACULTIES.
I HAVE POSITIONED THE SHIP AT A SAFE DISTANCE WHILE WE INVESTIGATE.

"WE HAVE SENT A PROBE INTO THE ANOMALY TO GATHER MORE DATA."
"IT IS MY HOPE THAT MORE INFORMATION WILL EXPLAIN THE CONNECTION TO YOUR UNUSUAL EXPERIENCE, CAPTAIN."

FIRST OFFICER'S LOG.
IT IS MY HOPE THAT THE CAPTAIN'S MOMENTARY CHANGE IN PERCEPTION WAS AS UNIQUE AS IT WAS UNUSUAL.
IF HIS CONDITION WORSENS, IT MAY REQUIRE US TO ABANDON OUR CURRENT COURSE AND RETURN THE CAPTAIN TO THE NEAREST STARBASE FOR TREATMENT.

IF OTHER MEMBERS OF THE CREW EXPERIENCE VISIONS SIMILAR TO THE CAPTAIN'S, IT SUGGESTS THAT THE ANOMALY IS IN FACT RESPONSIBLE.
WE MUST BALANCE THE HEALTH AND SAFETY OF THE CREW WITH OUR MISSION TO EXPLORE ANY UNUSUAL--
LIGHTS!

OH! I'M SORRY, HONEY, I DIDN'T KNOW YOU WERE HERE!
...LIEUTENANT UHURA?

LIGHTS!

MISTER SPOCK, WHAT ARE YOU DOING?!
NYOTA?

I'VE TOLD YOU BEFORE, SPOCK, YOU DON'T HAVE TO CALL ME "LIEUTENANT" WHEN WE'RE ALONE...

MY APOLOGIES. I SHOULD NOT BE HERE.
WHAT...?

WHY ARE YOU IN MY QUARTERS?
YOU...
...ARE *NOT* THE NYOTA I KNOW...
AND YOU ARE MOST CERTAINLY *NOT* ACTING LIKE THE SPOCK I *KNOW!*
SPOCK, WHAT'S WRONG?
I BELIEVE I AM EXPERIENCING A HALLUCINATION SIMILAR TO THE CAPTAIN'S.
0.4
0.5
0.6
0.7
0.8
0.9
I AM STILL ABOARD THE *ENTERPRISE*, AND YET... *NOT.*

WHAT'S HAPPENED TO ENGINEERING?!

AND WHO ARE YOU PEOPLE SUPPOSED TO BE?

YE'VE GOT TO BE KIDDING ME...

I BLINK AND EVERYTHING'S CHANGED!
WHAT'S WRONG, CHIEF?

WHAT'S ALL THIS?
WHAT ARE THESE...THESE *BUTTONS AND LIGHTS...*

WOULD SOMEBODY PLEASE TELL ME WHAT'S GOING ON?!

AAAH--!

HRRMP
GET AWAY FROM ME, YE WEE MONSTER!

THERE'S GOT TO BE AN EXPLANATION.
WE'VE ALL EXPERIENCED THE SAME STRANGE VISIONS. SOME OF US FOR MERE SECONDS, OTHERS FOR LONGER.
VISIONS OF A SHIP-- AN *ENTERPRISE*-- UNLIKE OUR OWN. A CREW WE DON'T RECOGNIZE.
ALL HYPOTHESES AS TO THE CAUSE ARE WELCOME.
IT SOUNDS LIKE WE ALL SAW THE SAME THING. AN *ENTERPRISE* UNLIKE OUR OWN.
A CREW WITH THE SAME NAMES BUT DIFFERENT FACES.
I DON'T THINK IT'S A SHARED DELUSION.
I THINK I KNOW WHAT'S GOING ON.

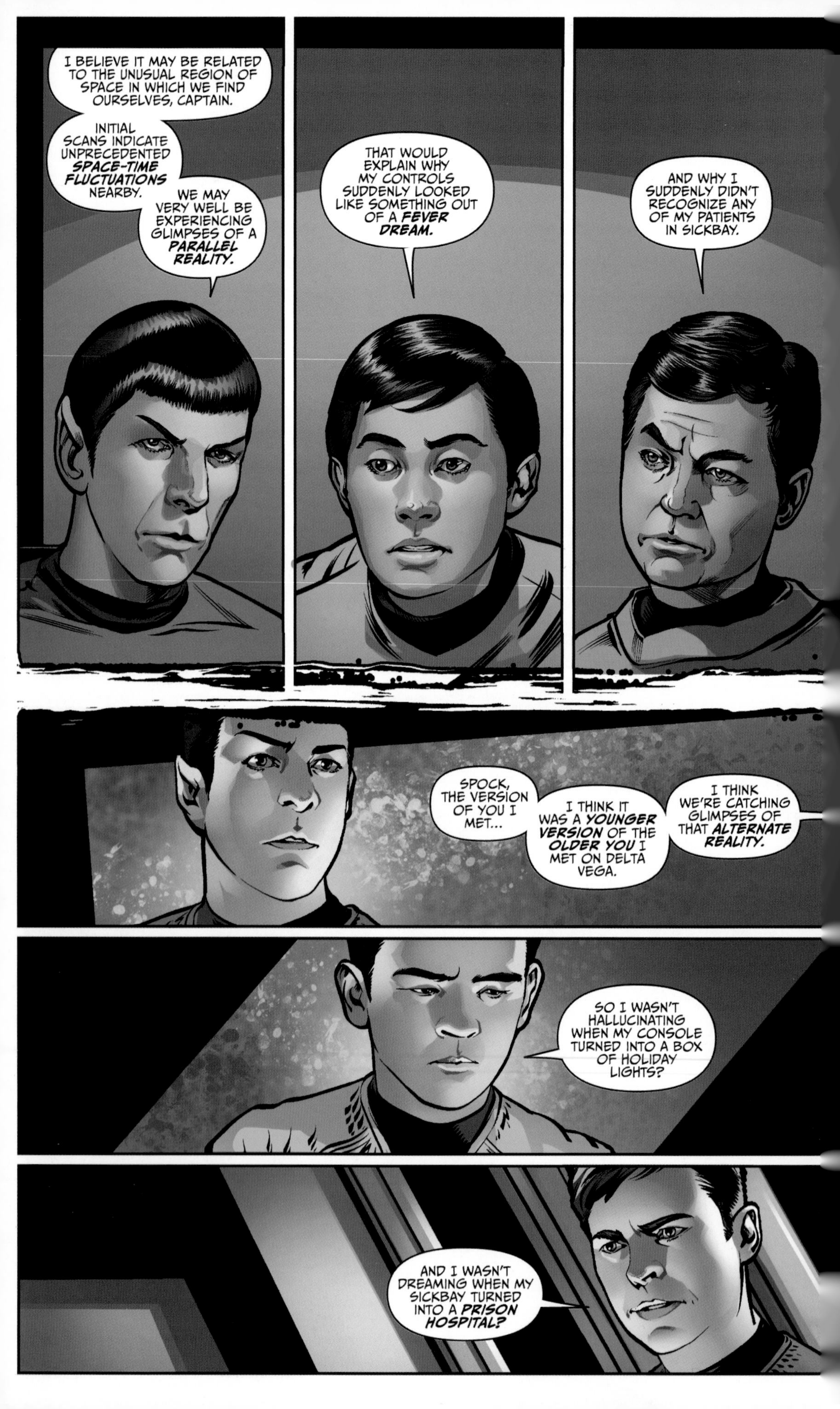

I BELIEVE IT MAY BE RELATED TO THE UNUSUAL REGION OF SPACE IN WHICH WE FIND OURSELVES, CAPTAIN.
INITIAL SCANS INDICATE UNPRECEDENTED SPACE-TIME FLUCTUATIONS NEARBY.
WE MAY VERY WELL BE EXPERIENCING GLIMPSES OF A PARALLEL REALITY.
THAT WOULD EXPLAIN WHY MY CONTROLS SUDDENLY LOOKED LIKE SOMETHING OUT OF A FEVER DREAM.
AND WHY I SUDDENLY DIDN'T RECOGNIZE ANY OF MY PATIENTS IN SICKBAY.
SPOCK, THE VERSION OF YOU I MET...
I THINK IT WAS A YOUNGER VERSION OF THE OLDER YOU I MET ON DELTA VEGA.
I THINK WE'RE CATCHING GLIMPSES OF THAT ALTERNATE REALITY.
SO I WASN'T HALLUCINATING WHEN MY CONSOLE TURNED INTO A BOX OF HOLIDAY LIGHTS?
AND I WASN'T DREAMING WHEN MY SICKBAY TURNED INTO A PRISON HOSPITAL?

WE HAVE TWO CHOICES. LEAVE NOW AND AVOID ANY FURTHER... DISRUPTIONS...OF OUR CONSCIOUSNESS...
...OR **STAY** AND LEARN EVERYTHING WE CAN ABOUT THIS PHENOMENON.
BRIDGE TO KEPTIN KIRK!

WHAT IS IT, MR. CHEKOV?
THE PROBE, SIR! WE HAVE RESTORED CONTACT WITH IT, BUT--

LEAVING THIS AREA MIGHT SAVE US FROM THESE VISIONS.
BUT IMAGINE WHAT MORE WE MIGHT LEARN IF WE **STAY.**
BRIDGE TO KEPTIN KIRK!

GO AHEAD, CHEKOV.
WE HAVE RESTORED CONTACT WITH THE PROBE, SIR, BUT--

"...IT'S NOT THE ONE WE SENT OUT!"
"...IT'S NOT THE ONE WE SENT OUT!"

CAPTAIN'S LOG, SUPPLEMENTAL. THE MYSTERY DEEPENS.
WELL, THIS PROBE CERTAINLY DIDN'T COME FROM OUR SHIP.
PERHAPS NOT IN THE STRICTEST SENSE, CAPTAIN.

CAPTAIN'S LOG, SUPPLEMENTAL. WE'VE RETRIEVED A STRANGELY FAMILIAR ITEM.
LOVELY, ISN'T IT? IT'S LIKE A LOST PROTOTYPE OF ONE OF OUR PROBES.
I'M OPEN TO THEORIES AS TO HOW IT ARRIVED, GENTLEMEN. AND WHAT HAPPENED TO THE PROBE WE SENT OUT.
I BELIEVE IT IS CONNECTED TO THE STRANGE HALLUCINATIONS WE HAVE BEEN EXPERIENCING.

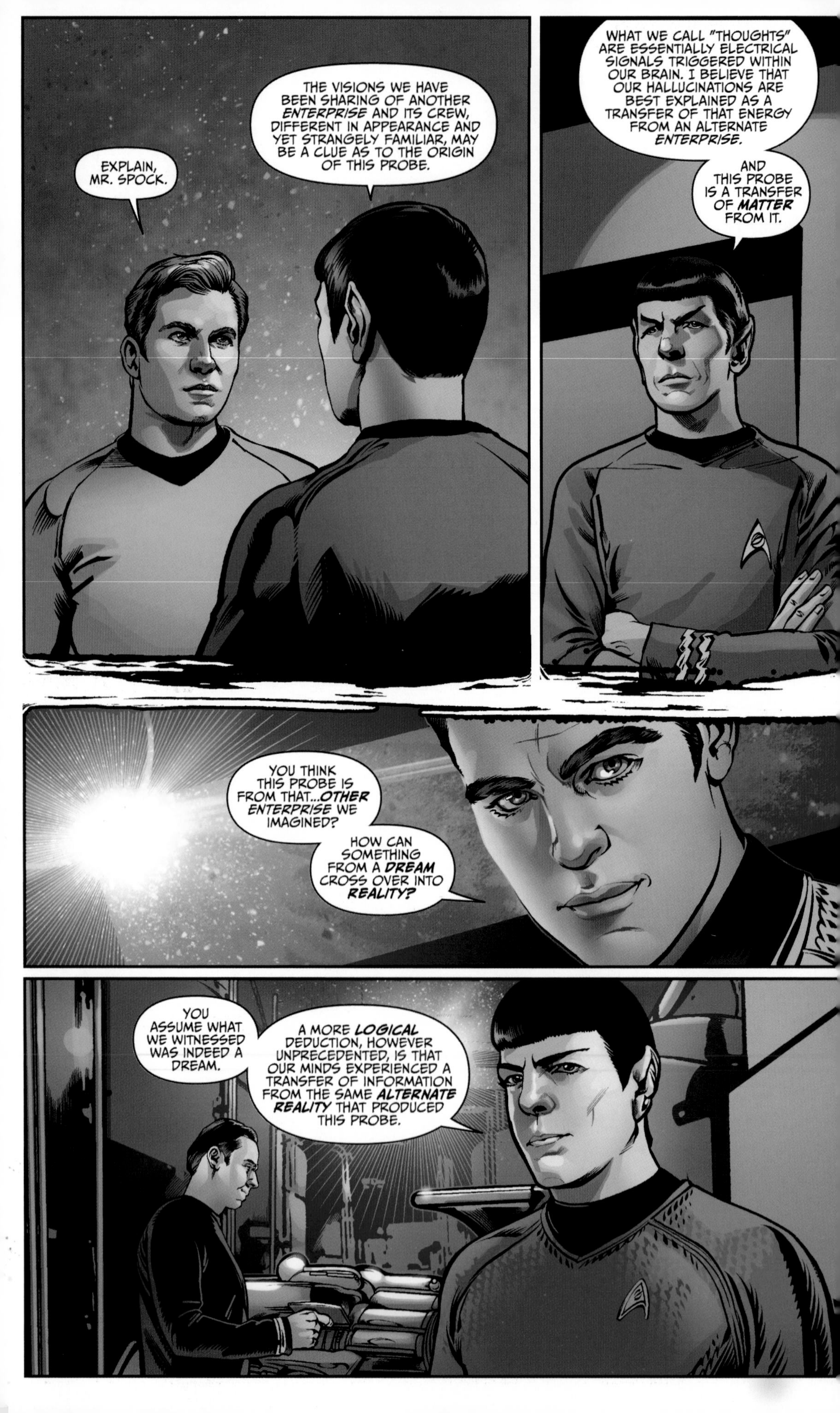
EXPLAIN, MR. SPOCK.
THE VISIONS WE HAVE BEEN SHARING OF ANOTHER *ENTERPRISE* AND ITS CREW, DIFFERENT IN APPEARANCE AND YET STRANGELY FAMILIAR, MAY BE A CLUE AS TO THE ORIGIN OF THIS PROBE.
WHAT WE CALL "THOUGHTS" ARE ESSENTIALLY ELECTRICAL SIGNALS TRIGGERED WITHIN OUR BRAIN. I BELIEVE THAT OUR HALLUCINATIONS ARE BEST EXPLAINED AS A TRANSFER OF THAT ENERGY FROM AN ALTERNATE *ENTERPRISE.*
AND THIS PROBE IS A TRANSFER OF ***MATTER*** FROM IT.
YOU THINK THIS PROBE IS FROM THAT...***OTHER ENTERPRISE*** WE IMAGINED?
HOW CAN SOMETHING FROM A ***DREAM*** CROSS OVER INTO ***REALITY?***
YOU ASSUME WHAT WE WITNESSED WAS INDEED A DREAM.
A MORE ***LOGICAL*** DEDUCTION, HOWEVER UNPRECEDENTED, IS THAT OUR MINDS EXPERIENCED A TRANSFER OF INFORMATION FROM THE SAME ***ALTERNATE REALITY*** THAT PRODUCED THIS PROBE.

ACH, NO... NOT AGAIN!

AYE, MONTGOMERY SCOTT! THAT'S STILL ME.
BUT WHO ARE YOU?!
MR. SCOTT--?

IT'S HAPPENING AGAIN...THE HALLUCINATIONS...
INDEED, CAPTAIN.

AND I BELIEVE THAT TIME IS RUNNING OUT TO SOLVE THIS MYSTERY.

SCOTTY--!
IT'S HAPPENING AGAIN! I'M BACK ON THIS... THIS...

...THIS SHINY WONDER!
AND THIS TIME, MR. SCOTT...

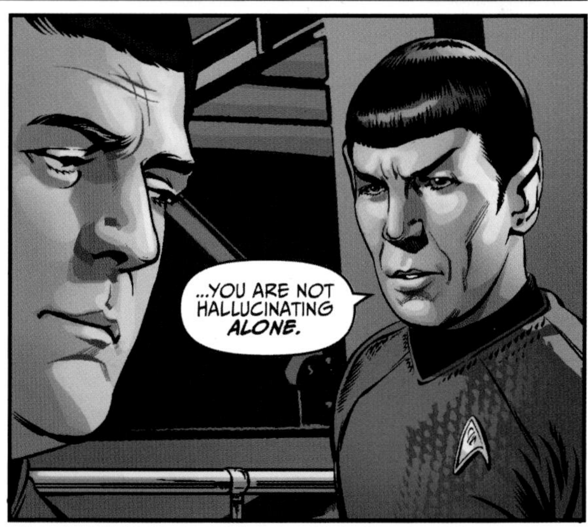
...YOU ARE NOT HALLUCINATING ALONE.

DAMNEDEST THING.
TO US YOU LOOK EXACTLY THE SAME...

...BUT YOU SAY YOU'RE ***SOMEONE ELSE*** INSIDE?
NOT SOMEONE ELSE, DOCTOR. I AM STILL SPOCK, BUT NOT THE ONE WITH WHOM YOU ARE FAMILIAR.
WELL, YOU CERTAINLY SHARE THE SAME CUDDLY DEMEANOR.

BRIDGE TO CAPTAIN KIRK. YOUR PRESENCE IS REQUESTED, SIR. IT'S ABOUT THE ANOMALY.
ON MY WAY, UHURA.

BRIDGE TO CAPTAIN. WE NEED YOU HERE, SIR.
SPOCK, SCOTTY, JOIN ME ON THE BRIDGE.
THEY'RE NOT GOING ANYWHERE UNTIL WE FIGURE OUT WHAT'S GOING ON!

BONES, NO MATTER ***WHICH*** SCOTTY AND SPOCK THEY ARE, THE ONLY WAY WE'RE GOING TO FIGURE THIS OUT--

--IS IF I HAVE ***BOTH THEIR BRAINS*** WORKING THE PROBLEM.

WE THINK IT'S ALIVE.
WE THEENK IT NEEDS HELP!
"HELP"?
I'M INCLINED TO ASK THE SAME OF IT...WHATEVER "IT" IS.
CHEKOV WAS ABLE TO DOWNLOAD DATA FROM THE PROBE WE RECOVERED.
BASED ON THE DATA'S NON-RANDOM SYNTACTIC STRUCTURE, I'VE SUCCEEDED INTO TRANSLATING IT INTO A RUDIMENTARY LANGUAGE.
THE ANOMALY IS A LIVING THING? WHY CAN'T WE SEE IT?
WE DON'T THINK IT HAS A CORPOREAL FORM, CAPTAIN. IT'S MORE LIKE...
...SENTIENT ENERGY.

IF IT'S TALKING TO US, WHAT IS IT SAYING?
ROUTING MY TRANSLATION THROUGH THE BRIDGE COMMS NOW, CAPTAIN.
A STRANGE NEW LIFE FORM...
WHAT MESSAGE HAVE YOU BEEN ABLE TO DECIPHER?
HAVE A LISTEN...

MINDS WE MEET
MINDS SAME
BUT NOT SAME
TRAPPED WITH YOU
WE CANNOT PASS
OUR INFINITE LOST
NCC-1701
NCC-1701

WELL THAT'S AS CLEAR AS TRITANIUM!
"OUR INFINITE LOST?" SURE, LET US JUST FIND THAT FOR YOU!
"TRAPPED..."
ENERGY BY ITS VERY NATURE IS INTENDED TO MOVE, TO CHANGE, NEVER ***STAGNANT...***
BUT LASHING OUT, IN THIS CASE, LIKE AN ANIMAL STUCK IN A ***TRAP.***

"MINDS," PLURAL, WOULD EXPLAIN WHY SOME OF US ARE EXPERIENCING ***PSYCHIC DISLOCATION,*** AS I AM NOW.
THE ANOMALY, IN ITS ATTEMPT TO COMMUNICATE, IS AFFECTING THE CREWS OF ***BOTH ENTERPRISES*** THAT HAVE ENCOUNTERED IT.
IT'S SCRAMBLING OUR SIGNALS.
SO THAT HALLUCINATION I HAD OF ANOTHER SHIP REALLY WAS A GLIMPSE OF ANOTHER REALITY.
AND THIS ANOMALY WOULD APPEAR TO EXIST IN ***BOTH AT ONCE.***

WELL IF IT'S "TRAPPED" WITH US, AS IT SAYS, WE NEED TO FIND A WAY TO ***FREE IT!***

MR. SPOCK AND MR. SCOTT INSIST THAT THEY ARE NOT THE SPOCK AND SCOTTY WE KNOW.

NOW MR. SULU IS EXPERIENCING THE SAME PHENOMENON.
BUT DESPITE THEIR DISCOMFORT, THEY INSIST ON DOING THEIR JOBS.
LAYOUT'S DIFFERENT, BUT I CAN FIGURE IT OUT...

I CAN TELL UHURA'S UNNERVED BY SPOCK'S BEHAVIOR. THERE'S A FAMILIARITY BETWEEN THE TWO THAT'S GONE NOW.
BUT THEY STILL WORK TOGETHER BETTER THAN ANY PAIR OF OFFICERS I'VE SEEN.

EVERYONE ONBOARD, ALL FACED WITH AS BIZARRE A PHENOMENON AS WE'VE EVER ENCOUNTERED, SHARES THE SAME GOAL.
SOLVE THE PROBLEM.

WE MAY HAVE FOUND A SOLUTION.

AFTER ANALYZING THE ENERGY SIGNATURES OBTAINED BY THE PROBE, WE BELIEVE THAT A CONTAINED MATTER/ANTI-MATTER DETONATION WILL TEAR A RIP IN THE FABRIC OF SPACE/TIME LARGE ENOUGH TO "FREE" THE ANOMALY CURRENTLY TRAPPED IN PARALLEL TIMELINES.

CAN WE RIG A TORPEDO TO DO SO?
AYE SIR. IT'S NOT THE DESIGN I'M FAMILIAR WITH, BUT TOGETHER WITH MR. SPOCK I CAN MAKE IT WORK.

SO OUR BEST COURSE OF ACTION IS GAMBLING ON A HYPOTHETICAL?

A WELL-REASONED ONE, GIVEN THE UNPRECEDENTED CHALLENGE WE FACE.
DON'T GET ME WRONG, SPOCK, I'M ALWAYS COMFORTABLE WITH HYPO--

WHAT THE--?!
KA-KOOOM
--THETICALS?!

CAPTAIN, THE BRIDGE--

THE CONTROLS--!

AI YI YI--!

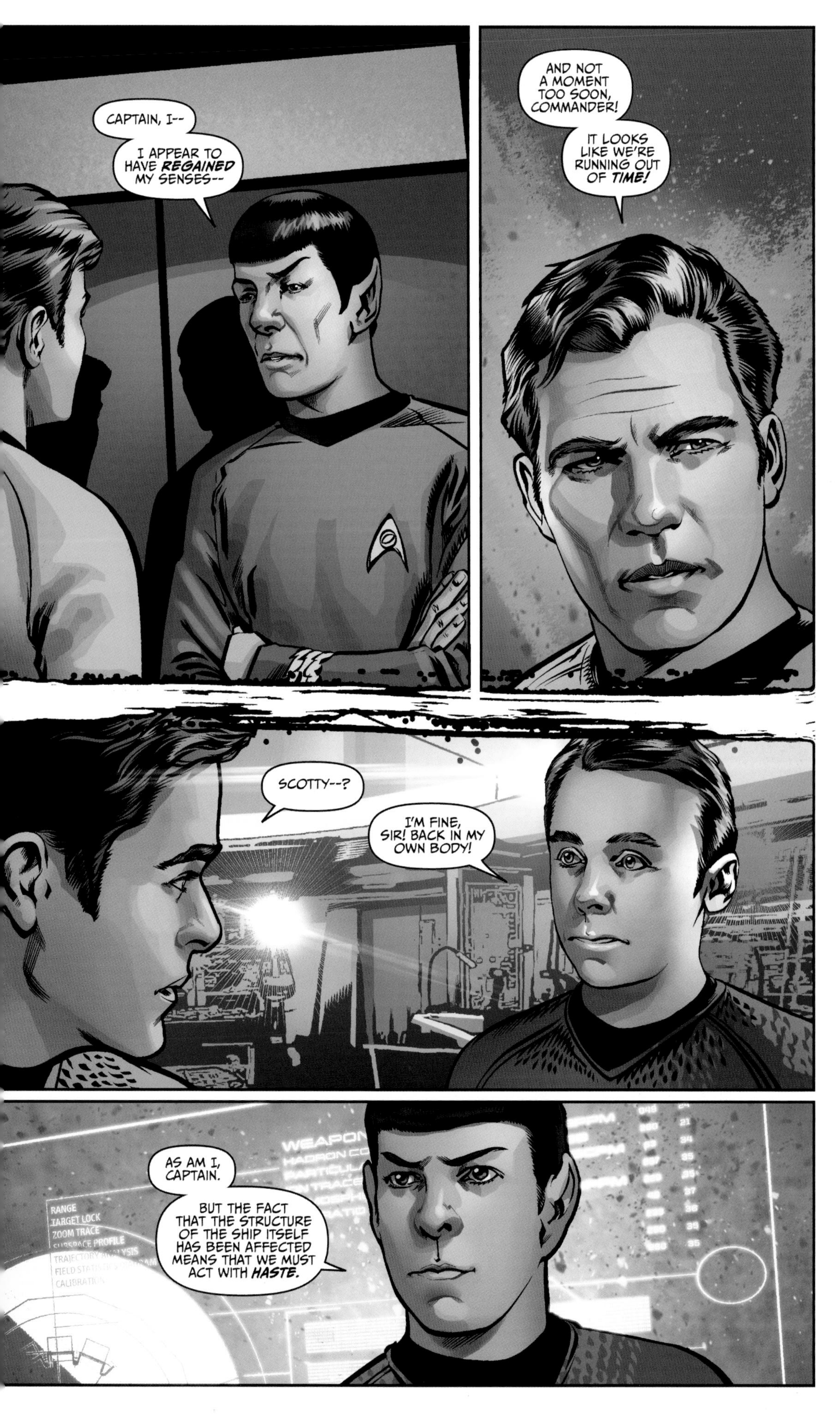
CAPTAIN, I--
I APPEAR TO HAVE ***REGAINED*** MY SENSES--
AND NOT A MOMENT TOO SOON, COMMANDER!
IT LOOKS LIKE WE'RE RUNNING OUT OF ***TIME!***
SCOTTY--?
I'M FINE, SIR! BACK IN MY OWN BODY!
AS AM I, CAPTAIN.
BUT THE FACT THAT THE STRUCTURE OF THE SHIP ITSELF HAS BEEN AFFECTED MEANS THAT WE MUST ACT WITH ***HASTE.***
RANGE
TARGET LOCK
ZOOM TRACE

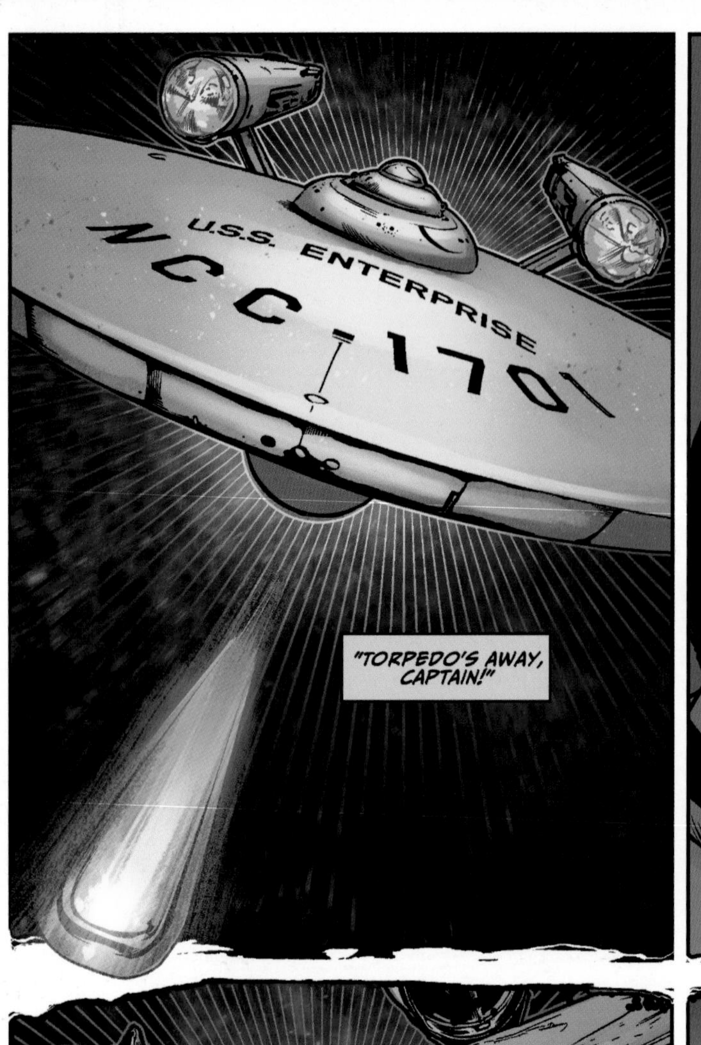
U.S.S. ENTERPRISE
NCC-1701
"TORPEDO'S AWAY, CAPTAIN!"

DETONATION IN 20, 19, 18....

"ON A STRAIGHT LINE TO WHERE WE LOST THE PROBE!"

DETONATION IN 3, 2, 1...

NCC-1701
U.S.S. ENTERPRISE

CAPTAIN'S LOG, SUPPLEMENTAL.
EVERYTHING APPEARS TO BE BACK TO NORMAL.
MS. RAND.
CAPTAIN.
CAPTAIN'S LOG, SUPPLEMENTAL.
WE'RE FREE OF WHATEVER HAD A HOLD OF US.
WE'VE HAD NO FURTHER CONTACT WITH THE ANOMALY WE ENCOUNTERED.

YOU'RE SURE, JIM? NO MORE HALLUCINATIONS?
I'M *FINE,* BONES.
I'LL LET YOU KNOW IF I HAVE SO MUCH AS AN EYE TWITCH.

ALTHOUGH I HAVE TO SAY, THE "BONES" I SAW IN THE OTHER SHIP APPEARED TO BE IN *EXCELLENT* PHYSICAL CONDITION.
SOUNDS LIKE HE'S NOT SPENDING ENOUGH TIME FOCUSED ON HIS *JOB.*

SO THIS "OTHER" ME...
SHE DIDN'T SO MUCH AS *WINK* AT YOU?
AS I SAID, SHE APPEARED TO HAVE NO ATTRACTION TOWARDS ME WHATSOEVER.

VULCANS CANNOT LIE.
RIIIIIIGHT.

EVEN WITH NORMALCY RETURNING, SOMETHING *FASCINATING* REMAINS.
IT APPEARS OUR DATABANKS NOW CONTAIN INFORMATION FROM *ANOTHER ENTERPRISE.*

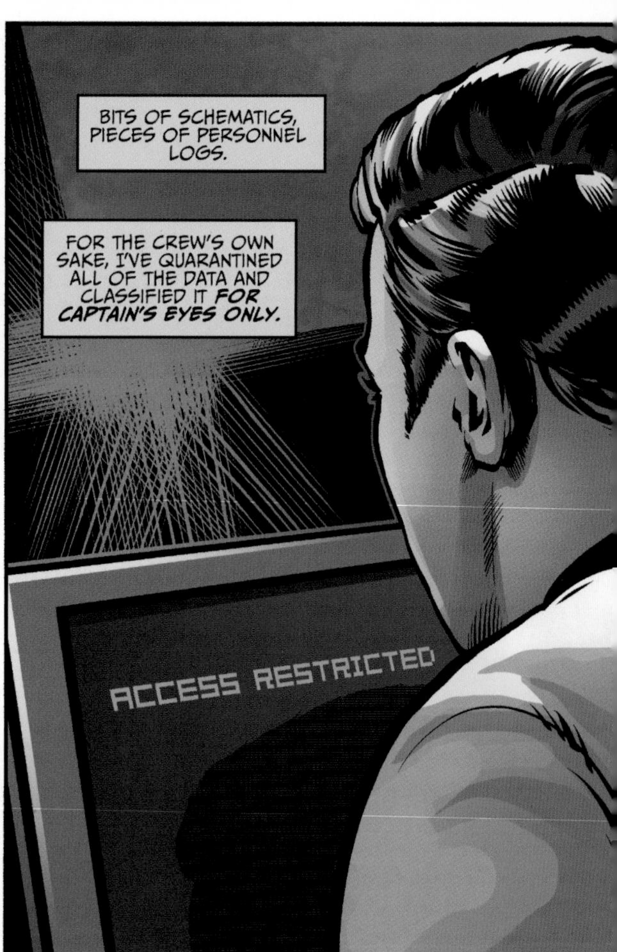
BITS OF SCHEMATICS, PIECES OF PERSONNEL LOGS.
FOR THE CREW'S OWN SAKE, I'VE QUARANTINED ALL OF THE DATA AND CLASSIFIED IT *FOR CAPTAIN'S EYES ONLY.*
ACCESS RESTRICTED

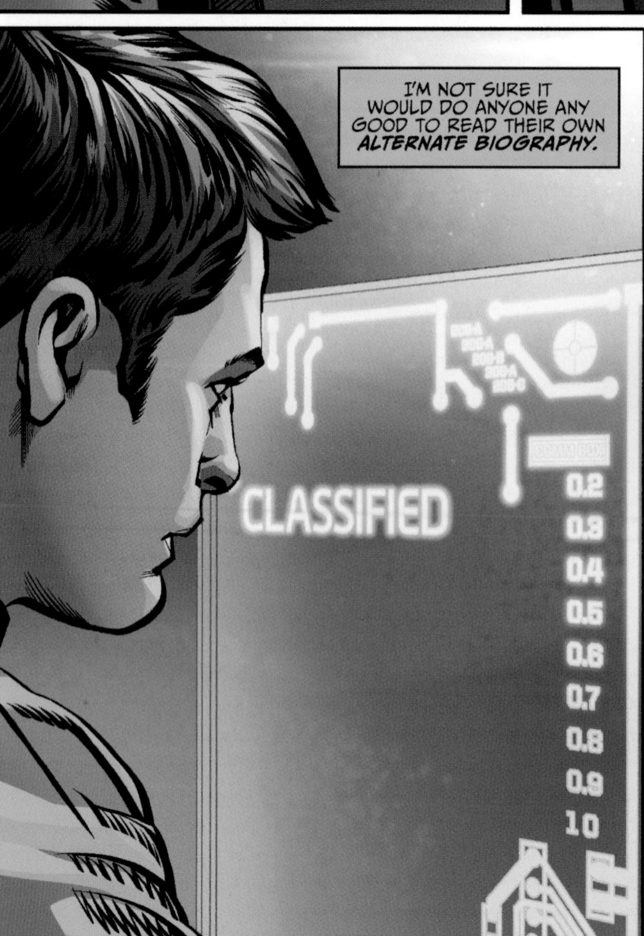
I'M NOT SURE IT WOULD DO ANYONE ANY GOOD TO READ THEIR OWN *ALTERNATE BIOGRAPHY.*
CLASSIFIED
0.2
0.3
0.4
0.5
0.6
0.7
0.8
0.9
1.0

I COULDN'T RESIST TAKING A LOOK BEFORE I LOCKED THEM AWAY.

ECHOES OF A LIFE I MIGHT HAVE LED.
BUT FOR ALL THE CHANGES...
FOR ALL THE DIFFERENCES IN HISTORY AND FATE...
...THERE REMAINS ONE COMMON TRUTH.
ONE SHARED BELIEF.

ONE MISSION.
NEVER THE END

Cover by Josh Adams, Colors by Adam Guzowski

Cover by J.K. Woodward

Cover by Tony Shasteen

Cover by John Watson

Cover by Tony Shasteen

Cover by J.K. Woodward

JOHNSON · SHASTEEN · MASTROLONARDO

STAR TREK®

"The **MIRACLE** is this:
The *more* we **SHARE**
the *more* we **HAVE**."
—Leonard Nimoy

SPOCK
FULLY POSABLE
ACTION FIGURE

Cover by Angel Hernandez, Colors by J.L. Del Rio

Cover by Tony Shasteen

Vintage Photo Cover

STAR TREK®

ROMULANS ON THE ATTACK!
A GALAXY IN TURMOIL!

HAILING...
DANGER!

Cover by Alberto Silva

Cover by Drew Moss, Colors by Adam Guzowski

Cover by Tony Shasteen